BEING ME

by
Lori Williams

Perfection Learning®

Cover Illustration: Greg Hargreaves

Dedication:

To my dear friend Toni Kenney—
Thanks for Joshua

For information, contact
Perfection Learning® Corporation
1000 North Second Avenue, P.O. Box 500
Logan, Iowa 51546-0500.
Phone: 1-800-831-4190
Fax: 1-800-543-2745
perfectionlearning.com

Paperback ISBN 0-7891-6024-2
Cover Craft® ISBN 0-7569-1372-1
1 2 3 4 5 6 PP 07 06 05 04 03

About the Author

Lori Williams was born the youngest of six children in the small farming community of El Campo, Texas. Both of her parents were teachers, and they never lost an opportunity to teach their children something new. Even family vacations became extended lessons in geography and history.

Williams received an English degree from the University of Houston. She has taught at the junior high level and at an alternative high school. She currently teaches English and reading at an academy for incarcerated boys in Hondo, Texas.

Even as a child, Williams loved to write. She wrote short stories, poetry, and even letters for her family and friends. Being a mother and teacher of teens has given her an appreciation of the teenage voice and the inspiration to write adolescent fiction. "I hope that in each story I write, young people will recognize something of themselves and perhaps gain fresh perspectives about the common nature of people. We are all a little strange, a little confused, a little insecure. It's our differences that make us interesting and our similarities that make us tolerable."

chapter 1

August

School of brick. Metal doors.
Simple people. Stupid wars.
Ordered kingdom. Not serene.
Many subjects. Empty Queen.

Joshua

Tuesday
August 20
Sky

My name is Sky, and I'm the prettiest girl in the seventh grade. I'm not conceited. Really, I'm not. I'm just brutally honest. I have silky blonde hair, ice-blue eyes, and an absolutely perfect body. I work on my looks. I do Tae-Bo three times a week, drink diet soda, and pack a salad for lunch every single day. While all of these other girls are fighting off pimples and cellulite, I'm fighting off boys.

All the guys love me. But here at Prescott, there are only a few that are worth my time. If a guy wants to talk to me, he has to: be fine, come from the right kind of family, and know how to dress. Finding someone who meets all three criteria certainly narrows a girl's prospects. I've liked John Keeler since the fifth grade. He's on our "list" of acceptable guys, even though his family doesn't quite qualify. They live in a middle-class neighborhood and drive boring cars. But his dad is a college professor, and Daddy says that's an honorable profession, even though professors don't make much money.

John was my boyfriend last year, and he will be my boyfriend again this year. Only, he doesn't know it yet. For the moment, he's all wrapped up in Sage Mobley. They're inseparable. Sage is a dork. She wears hiking boots and has a pageboy haircut. A pageboy, for God's sake! And, get this—she reads books. Not magazines like *Seventeen*. Books. John reads books too. He is a bit of a geek. But he's great-looking, so that's okay. Sage, on the other hand, is a schoolgirl. Someone needs to tell her that we're, like, in a new millennium. I can't believe John hangs out with her. What does she have that I don't? When we broke up, he told me I was "shallow." God only knows what that's supposed to mean.

Oh, well. What was I writing about? Oh, about myself. I wear great clothes. My mother takes me shopping in the city at least once a month. Only we don't go to those cheesy stores that all the other kids go to. We go to Saks and Bloomingdale's. I would die if I showed up at school wearing something that another kid had on. Especially if it was some loser from one of the groups I don't hang with.

I choose my friends carefully. They're either with me or against me, if you know what

I mean. We've all been in the same crowd since kindergarten. Except for Joanne. She moved here from the city last year. She's coming along, though at first we had to give her a few tips on who's who. For example, she was actually hanging around with Tiffany Andrews—*in public*. Tiffany is a reject! She either scurries around school with her nose to the ground like a little lab rat or has her nose stuck in a book. And oh, my God—you should see her hair!

Once we explained to Joanne what hanging out with losers can do to your social life, she told old Tiff to bounce. We chose Joanne to be part of our group because her parents are members of the country club. Her dad is a doctor, and her mom used to be a fashion consultant for some pretty high-class clothing stores. Other than her attraction to nerds, the only other strike against Joanne was her race. She isn't white. I had absolutely no problem with it, but you know, the other girls are a bit cliquish. I had to convince them that it was okay. Joanne is Spanish. I find that rather romantic—you see, I'm French myself.

The rest of my friends are: Candice, Julia, and Courtney. Sometimes one of them does something that requires the rest of us to shun her for a while, but we always include the offender again after she has served the sentence for her *faux pas*. That's French for "social screw-up" in case you didn't know. Just some of the faux pas that can get one of the gang into trouble are: wearing clothes from cheap department stores, associating with dorks, hooking up with a guy that isn't on our approved list, or rubbing me the wrong way.

I'm the leader of our little clique. Every group needs one, and I'm the most qualified. My friends are all okay, of course, but Momma says I'm more sophisticated than the rest of the kids at my school. So, naturally, I should be the leader.

As for the other groups at school, they really don't even deserve space in my journal, but I'll include them just for the sake of showing you the difference between us and them. We are at the top of the seventh-grade ladder, so to speak, at Prescott Junior High. Beneath us, *several* rungs down, are the "wanna-bes." These are the girls who watch our every move and try desperately and, of course, unsuccessfully to imitate us. They are also the girls who will try out for cheerleading and get jealousy votes from the other losers. Not enough votes to win, just enough to give them false hope for next year. Below the wanna-bes are the poor kids whose parents spend every cent they have to send them to school in new clothes every August. They could almost pass as one of us in those first few weeks of school, but by November, they're easy to recognize. That's when their new clothes have faded, their haircuts have grown into unrecognizable naps, and their jewelry has turned green. Then after Christmas, they come back all nice and dressed up and start the process all over again.

There are others, of course. The thugs, who are a little scary because they have a whole different set of styles and rules that I don't even begin to understand. The freaks, who actually *try* to look like they bought their clothes at garage sales. Freaks will throw on any old assortment of odds and ends from fishnet hose to combat boots. And the geeks, who don't give a fig what they look like as long as the teacher is patting them on their eggheads and telling them how freaking smart they are.

This is Prescott Junior High. Despite its large population of undesirables, this is my kingdom, and I am the princess.

Wednesday
August 21
Tiffany

My parents named me Tiffany because they thought I'd grow up to be elegant. I didn't. If they had me to name all over again, they'd probably pick something hideous like Drucilla. I wish I were a Tiffany. I'm not. When people think of Tiffany, they think of beautiful blondes with wide blue eyes or fancy restaurants where lovers meet for breakfast.

My hair is blonde. But not movie-star or fashion-model blonde. It's a dingy, dusty blonde. Grandma calls it "dishwater" blonde. How gross is that? Dishwater blonde—like that disgusting water my mother soaks the scalloped potato dish in overnight. That's my hair—gross and disgusting—dishwater blonde. To make matters worse, I have hundreds of stray strands that stick out everywhere. My mother says that's from yanking my ponytail holders out and not brushing my hair before bed. Oh well, who cares if my hair is a mess? I don't have time to primp, and even if I did, it wouldn't help the rest of me because other than my nappy hair,

I'm too skinny, and I have an overbite. The overbite can be fixed, according to my mother and my orthodontist, but not until this summer. Until then, I'm Drucilla, the buck-toothed, dirty dishwater kid.

I'm writing this as a school assignment. Miss Laughinghouse says that we each have to write at least one journal entry a week. She swears she won't read them—just "skim through" to see if we did the work. Miss Laughinghouse says, "Journaling will improve your writing skills and help you get in touch with yourselves." She's flaky. She's a new teacher, that's why. New teachers aren't predictable like the old ones. When they've been around long enough, they give up on all these great teaching ideas and stick to textbooks and worksheets.

Anyway, today was the second day of the seventh grade. I don't like school. I like to read, and I like to learn stuff, but I hate school. I've hated it since the first day of kindergarten. That's because ever since kindergarten, embarrassing things have happened to me almost on a daily basis. I trip and fall on my face, spit flies out of my mouth when I talk, toilet paper gets stuck on my shoe . . .

You name it, it's happened to me. Take today for instance.

Miss Laughinghouse let us move our desks into whatever position we wanted. She told us that "a classroom should be a non-restrictive environment where kids can feel free to express themselves." They expressed themselves, all right. They threw paper when her back was turned, wrote stupid stuff like "Jane luvs Joe" on the chalkboard, and stuck "kick me" signs on poor old Joshua Melton.

I moved my desk into the corner and turned it to face the wall. That way, I didn't have to look at anyone other than Garfield—he's on a poster next to my desk that says "Apathy Is Not an Option." Teachers are always plastering their rooms with posters that have witty sayings most kids couldn't understand without the aid of a dictionary.

Anyway, I was writing an article on "How To Make Deviled Eggs." When I write or read or anything, I sit on one leg and lean way over close to my paper. I need glasses. Last year, the nurse sent a note home with me to tell my mom that my vision is lousy. I threw the note away. That's all I need, to be Drucilla the *four-eyed*, buck-toothed, dirty dishwater kid. Okay, so I was leaning way forward, and I didn't know it, but my underwear was above my hip-huggers by about three inches. I know, because when I got home, I contorted myself in front of the bathroom mirror to see just how bad it had been.

So, I was sitting there with my underwear hanging out, and Jimmy Rojas noticed. Before long, he'd alerted the entire class. I heard all the snickering going on behind me but chose to ignore it. I was secretly hoping that old Jerky Josh was talking to his shoe or something and that's what the commotion was about. Joshua Melton has "problems." Sometimes he talks to himself, and he's always organizing his pencils, rubber bands, or whatever into neat little rows on his desk. Kids have picked on him since kindergarten. I hate it when they do that, but then again, if they weren't picking on poor old Jerky Josh, they'd probably be picking on me.

Anyway, I didn't know what the deal was until I got up to leave and the note came loose from wherever they'd stuck it—my underwear, the desk, my shirt? It said, "Tiffany wears granny panties." I was mortified.

Thursday
August 22
Joanne

This is the first week of a new school year, and the only homework I have so far is this journal entry. I told Mama that I was doing homework. That way, if the phone is for me, she'll tell whoever it is that I can't talk. I'm avoiding my friends.

We moved to this town last year. Until then, I had lived in the city. Since I moved here, I've become someone that I'm not sure I really like. First I'll tell you about the old me, and then I'll tell you about the new me.

I grew up in the city, as I said. Papa and Mama are both from Mexico. Papa was a poor kid who was lucky enough to attend a decent public school. He was given a grant for college and became an orthopedic surgeon. Mama came from a wealthy family in Mexico City. She studied fashion design. Until I was born, she worked as a fashion consultant for expensive clothing stores. Papa and Mama met in college and got married. When they graduated, they moved from Mexico to the United States.

At my old school, I was a top student. I received awards every single year for academic excellence. I had lots of friends. When we moved here, I didn't feel like I fit in. Most of these kids have known each other since kindergarten, and they aren't used to new kids coming along and joining in. For a while, I hung around with a girl named Tiffany. She was a loner too. Then Sky and her crowd noticed me. That's when I started to change.

At first, I really liked being part of Sky's crowd. I felt flattered. I never stopped to wonder why I was being asked to join the sacred club. I suppose that it had something to do with my parents' wealth, which in a town this size seems considerable.

For a while, everything seemed great. I had friends that everyone admired. Even the teachers treat the five of us a little differently. We're the ones who get to run errands or do special projects. Being cheerleaders and members of student council and yearbook committee are all "givens" for us. We had fun too. Sky was always arranging sleepovers at one of our houses. We'd try on one another's clothes, give manicures, read magazines, or edit the ever-changing list of acceptable boys.

But now, little things that I hadn't noticed before have started to get to me. For one thing, Sky tells everyone that I'm Spanish. I suppose that she thinks Spanish is European and therefore somehow rates above Mexican. She's always joking around about our group being "international." Her great-great-grandmother was French. She says that being Spanish makes me "exotic." The worst part of this is that I've never bothered to correct her. I'm not Spanish—I'm Mexican American. To say that I'm Spanish is like saying a twelfth-generation American is British.

I've never even told Sky, or any of them, that my parents were born and raised in Mexico. I never let on that I speak fluent Spanish. Why? Because I don't want to be different in that way. Sky makes jokes about the other Mexican kids right in front of me. She calls them "wets." Even though it's obvious that I'm Mexican, Sky's made it okay by telling herself and everyone else that I'm Spanish because that fits more neatly into her vision of things. Sky creates her own reality.

Another thing that bugs me is that I find myself going along with Sky when I know she's doing things that hurt other people. Take

Tiffany, for example. I see her in the hallway and my face burns with shame because of the way I dropped her on Sky's demand. Tiffany was a true friend. I could be myself around her. Then I turned around and betrayed her. I not only sold her out for friendship with Sky, I mocked her with the others. I'm a Judas.

I feel trapped by my friends. Trapped into being someone that I'm not. I act stupid and shallow because that's the way they like me. I even changed the way I talk. I say stupid things like "Duh," "For real?" and "Whatever." Our conversations go like this:

"Hey, Joanne. What's up?"

"Like, not much. How 'bout you?"

"Just bought a, like, really cool purse."

"For real?"

"Yeah, from Macy's. And it was, like, really expensive."

"Like, duh! How much?"

And on, and on, and on. We never really say anything. So here I am, a brainless turncoat. My 30 pieces of silver have bought me an allotted place in Sky's "kingdom." I'm to be beautiful, stylish, exotic, and empty.

MONDAY
AUGUST 26
BRANDON

I hate to write. I also hate to read. I hate language class in general. Now I have this lame journal project that's due at the end of every month. Miss Laughinghouse swears she's not gonna read this crap. We'll see.

School can be one of two things: boring or fun. If it's gonna be fun, I gotta make it that way. Teachers go out of their way to make it as dull as possible. That's where I come in. I liven things up a little. Like yesterday, when I smudged chalk all over my hand and left a print on Miss Laughinghouse's stool. She was wearin' black pants, which made it perfect. There she went, bustling down the hall with my handprint right on her butt.

Not that I don't like Laughinghouse. She's okay. First of all, I can do pretty much whatever I want in her class. Second, she's the only teacher at this school that's worth givin' a second look. Probably 'cause she's the only teacher that isn't old enough to be my grandma. Yeah, Miss Laughinghouse, you're pretty hot. I'd like to . . . Oh, better not say just in case you're peekin' through our entries.

Tuesday
August 27
Sage

Another year of school. I didn't get to do one single thing that I wanted to do over summer break. Mom had promised to take us camping in the hill country. She also said that we might spend a week at the lake. I should have known that the camping trip would fall through. I can't picture Mom sitting around a fire or sleeping in a tent. How could she possibly go without electricity? No makeup mirrors, blow dryers, or curling irons. It would be too much to ask for her to spend time with just us kids, out in the wilderness with no man within a hundred miles.

We did go to the lake. But only because Mom had a crush on the guy that owns property next to the cabin we rented. A crush. Moms aren't supposed to have crushes. That's what she calls it though, whenever she gets all head-over-heels with some new guy.

My parents are divorced. They have been for more than two years. Until the divorce, Mom was just like other moms: cooking, cleaning, and sewing patches on my little sister's Brownie uniform. Then Dad up and left her for some woman he met at work. She was devastated. I suppose that's why she acts the way she does. Carly, that's my dad's girlfriend, is younger than Mom—by about ten years. Now Mom's trying to be a teenager again because she thinks that's what men want. She dresses in clothes that are too tight and show too much skin. She got her navel pierced, and she uses words like "hip" and "cool." Just yesterday when John came over, she slapped him a high-five. It's embarrassing.

So we went to the lake but only stayed two days. It was great while it lasted. Brandy and I swam and hiked around in the woods. Mom brought snacks to the deck, and we sat around telling funny stories. It was great, even though I noticed Mom glancing over to the neighbor's house every few minutes and getting jumpy whenever she heard a car out on the access road. Then it happened. The moment Mom had *really* been waiting for. She was all dolled up lying in her bikini on one of the deck chairs out front. Brandy and I were playing a game of Battleship at the picnic table when we heard a car door slam and a woman laughing. It was Mom's crush arriving for his weekend at the lake. Only he wasn't alone. He was with this drop-dead beautiful redhead. They waved at us as they walked up the path to his cabin: arm in arm, all giggles. Mom smiled and waved back, but you could tell that the wind had been knocked right out of her sails.

After that, we stopped having fun. Mom got snappy, so Brandy and I were afraid to laugh or talk too loud. That afternoon, she started packing up our stuff and announced that she needed to "go back to town and get some things done around the house." So we left after only two days. We were supposed to stay for a whole week. On the ride home, no one said a word. Brandy was fighting tears the whole way, but I was just mad. Why did everything have to be about Mom? She hadn't wanted to spend time with us at all. She'd planned the whole trip around some stupid guy who barely knew she existed. When that fell through, the whole vacation was ruined.

When we got back to town, Mom got all dressed up and went "out for a while." I was left at home to baby-sit Brandy. We waited up for her until 11:00. Then Brandy fell asleep, and I lay for hours wondering if Mom had gotten into a wreck or something. I must have dozed off, because I woke up when I heard her bump into the coffee table on the way to her bedroom. It was 2:00 in the morning.

I miss the old pre-divorce mom. I also miss my dad, even though deep down I kind of hate him for what he did to Mom and to me and Brandy. On the weekends that we go to his house, he's all lovey-dovey with Carly. It makes me sick. I picture Mom, alone and desperately trying to find someone to fill the hole he left behind, while he's as happy as a clam.

Carly's 25, but she acts like she's 10. She tries to be my friend. Sure, she can be fun sometimes. She likes hiking and boating and all of the stuff that I like. But every time I find myself liking Carly, I picture Mom. I'll never let myself get close to the woman that stole my dad. Even though Mom is selfish and embarrassing sometimes, she does deserve some loyalty. After all, she did sew on all those Brownie badges, make Halloween costumes, cook our meals, and braid our hair.

Wednesday
August 28
Tiffany

I have Mrs. Clark for social studies. Most people would think that's a bad thing. Everyone who has an older brother or sister was warned about "The Tank." She got that nickname because she was in the army during the Vietnam War. She's strict. No one gets picked on in Mrs. Clark's class. If someone cuts up, she says, "Boy, you better watch it or I'll skin you alive and hang you out to dry." She could do it too. She's huge. I like her. She tells interesting stories, and she doesn't care one bit what people think of her. She's also the only teacher that didn't pat me on the back the first day of school and say, "Hello, Tiffany. I taught your sister Marilyn."

Marilyn's dead—killed in a car wreck her freshman year of college. She was a lot older than me, eight years to be exact. Everyone loved Marilyn: teachers, parents, kids, boys—everyone. She was perfect. When she died, Mom went off the deep end.

We got the phone call at 2:00 in the morning on April 13, almost a year and a half ago. Mom freaked. I woke up to all of the commotion and went to my parents' room. Dad was getting dressed, just like he was going to work, except he had this horrible look on his face. He was all white, and his lips were clinched together like he was afraid if he relaxed his mouth a little, he'd start to cry. Mom was sitting on the side of the bed in her robe with a pillow over her face stifling what would have been screams—if my mother were the type of woman who could scream.

No, they weren't screams exactly, just one horrible, heart-wrenching sound after another. Sounds like I heard one time in a restaurant when a baby got the skin of his belly caught in one of those alligator clips they put on high-chair straps. His poor daddy couldn't get the clip undone, and the kid just kept wailing until he looked like he was going to pass out.

It's funny how everything can change in a split second. Perfect, straight-A, prom queen Marilyn, pulls out in front of a truck on Highway 90, 150 miles from home, and suddenly we're in hell. Mom couldn't function. She just sat around and cried all the time. No one could mention Marilyn's name without sending her into orbit. About a month after it happened, I went into Marilyn's room to get some notebook paper. She always kept a stack in her desk for when she'd come home from college on weekends. Mom caught me going through Marilyn's desk, and she went nuts. She yelled at me to leave Marilyn's things alone. I ran and locked myself in my room. I cried for hours that night.

After that, Mom locked Marilyn's room. All of Marilyn's things are still in there like she's going to pop in the door some Saturday morning and announce that she's going to her room to study for midterms. I don't understand Mom. Marilyn's dead, and I can't even use her stupid notebook paper.

Anyway, Dad went on with life. But he had that same horrified look on his face that he'd had the night they got "the news." He couldn't talk to Mom, so he kept busy in the garage every evening. He organized his tools, scrubbed the oil spots from the concrete, even dusted the rafters. That went on for months. Then they started going to counseling.

Evidently, the counselor told Mom that talking about Marilyn would help. She talks about her pretty often, I'll tell you. That's okay and all, if it helps Mom, but I hate it when she compares me to Marilyn. "Why don't you have some friends over once and a while Tiffany? When Marilyn was your age, she had tons of friends." "Why don't you get your hair cut like Marilyn had hers? It was so cute on her!" Stuff like that. Sometimes I think Mom wants to recreate Marilyn. She thinks that if she concentrates hard enough, I'll morph from the buck-toothed, dirty dishwater kid into the gorgeous prom queen. Poor Mom.

She asked me yesterday if I'd made any friends this year. I tell her all the time that I have plenty of friends at school; I just don't ask them over or talk on the phone because I'd rather not be bothered. I even make up stories that these "friends" tell me at lunch. I say, "I sat with so-and-so, and they said such-and-such." This gets Mom off my back for a while, but I really think she suspects I'm lying. She just looks at me kind of sad and puzzled. I know she's thinking, "Marilyn had dozens of friends at your age."

I did have a best friend for a while last year. Her name was Joanne. The only reason that she was my friend in the first place was because she'd just moved here from someplace else and she didn't have a soul to hang out with. Our science teacher made us study buddies, so we were forced into each other's company. We were friends for a whole two months. She even stayed over at my house one night, and we watched movies and ate pizza. Mom was so excited about me having company that she blew a big wad of cash at the grocery store on snacks and soda water. Having giggling girls in the house probably reminded her of the good-old days when Marilyn's friends flocked in to raid the fridge all breathy and beautiful after basketball practice.

Anyway, it didn't last. Joanne found new friends, and they told her what a geek I am. She dumped me like a hot potato. She even joined in and laughed at some crack they made when I walked through the courtyard one day during lunch. I wonder what she told them about me. I'd told Joanne all of my deep, dark secrets: how I hate the way I look and how I wish I could be pretty like my older sister had been. I even told her that I wish boys would like me. I bet that gave them all something to laugh about. Now every time I pass Joanne in the hall, my face gets all hot, and I look at the floor or turn a corner. She tries to be nice and say hello *if* her friends aren't around. I avoid her. In fact, I despise her.

Thursday
August 29
Sky

Saturday night is the "Back to School Bash." I can't wait. Last year, when I was in the sixth grade, we weren't allowed to attend any of the school dances. This year, I get to be the belle of the ball on several occasions: the Back to School Bash, Fall Festival, the Valentine's Dance, and Spring Madness. FINALLY, someplace to go where I can really dress up.

I've been thinking all week about what I want to wear. Momma says that we can go into the city tomorrow night and buy a new dress for the occasion. She and Daddy had a blowout over it. He says that Momma spends way too much on my wardrobe. She says—and she's right—that if I don't dress nice, I won't attract the right kind of people. Momma won, as always. Tomorrow, right after school, we're off to the mall. I'm going to look *so* good at that dance, John Keeler will just die.

chapter 2

September

Honored game. Screaming crowd.
Struggling athletes. Parents proud.
Here's the mascot. Tattered mask.
Who portrays him? Shouldn't ask.
Kingdom's crumbling. Unforeseen.
In the costume is the Queen.

Joshua

Monday
September 2
Tiffany

For this journal entry, I'll use one of Miss Laughinghouse's writing prompts: What I hate most about school is _______________.

What I hate most about school is kids, if you want to know the truth. They're all boring and stupid. They talk about the same old stuff every day. I can narrow my classmate's conversations into three categories: who loves who, who hates who, and who's who. Boring! I don't really care how I look or whether the stupid boys at this school like me. All of these kids are STUPID!

I forgot to mention that the Spanish Club was responsible for hosting the Back to School Bash on Saturday night. This meant that not only did I have to go to the dance, I had to serve punch and cookies all night. Watching all of those idiots trying to outdo one another made me want to crack up. From my vantage point behind the snack table, it looked like something right out of one of those hokey teenage movies they show on cable every Friday night. There were the nerds all crowded up against the wall talking about the square root of pi or something, the thugs with their pants pulled halfway down to their knees working terribly hard to look cool, the wanna-be popular girls giggling and walking to the bathroom every five minutes just so they could sashay past the boys by the water fountain, and the beautiful people—Sky, Courtney, Joanne, Candice, and Julia. They were the most pathetic of all, if you ask me. They just stood there around Sky as if she were the center of their universe, hanging on every stuck-up, inane, airhead comment that she made.

Sky was outrageous! She walked in wearing a backless dress that fit so tight you could see every curve in her overdeveloped body. I thought Principal Williams would flip out, but he didn't say a word. Sky got to stay for the dance, even though she was committing at least a dozen student-dress code violations. If it had been some slob from a poor family trying to sneak in the door dressed like Madonna, Williams would have thrown her out on her ear. But not Sky. She walked in like she owned the place, and no one said a word. Probably because her parents think they *do* own the place. They're always donating money for band uniforms or new library books. Just last week, her mom had her face plastered all over the front page of the paper for donating funds for a new sign to put out front. Williams is definitely on the take.

Anyway, I managed to avoid talking to anyone the whole night. I didn't trip and fall over the snack table or do anything else horrible that would draw attention to myself. I didn't even look at anyone. I just handed out punch and cookies and sent everyone graciously on their way. Joanne tried to strike up a conversation with me while her friends were off primping in the bathroom. I ignored her and went to work scooping ice from the cooler into the punch bowl. I wanted to tell her something, but I couldn't bring myself to say it.

I wanted to tell her that I'm not as stupid as her new friends. That I can see through the petty game she's playing. In Spanish class she pretends she doesn't even know how to say *Buenos días*, when I know she can jabber away in Spanish better than Santa Anna himself. She wants everyone to think she's stupid for some reason, and it's working.

She is stupid. Stupid for selling out to a bunch of snobs, stupid for thinking that I'll ease her conscience by forgiving her, stupid for thinking that stupid is attractive to anyone other than stupid people.

Everyone is talking about the dance. I was stunning. My dress was pale blue with royal blue sequins. Momma said that it accentuated my beautiful eyes. It was short, way above the fingertip rule outlined in our student handbook. It was also backless. The dress, my nails, my hair appointment, and the other necessary accessories cost a fortune. Daddy had a fit. I heard him and Momma arguing about it for over an hour. Why he's so stingy with money all of a sudden is just beyond me.

As I was saying, my body is incredible, and the dress did me justice, even if I do say so myself. I wore my hair piled up and had it curled into a thousand ringlets. It took the hairdresser two hours to do it. Then I made her start all over because it didn't look quite right. She had it too bunched toward the front, which, anyone with any sense would know, doesn't play up my Grecian profile. Momma says it is just impossible to find a competent hairdresser in a town this size. Next time, I'll have it done in the city where beauticians know the latest styles.

I arrived at the dance about 30 minutes after it started. That's a rule I live by: show up a bit late. That way, you can make an entrance. If you show up when everyone else does, you run the risk of getting mixed up in the crowd, and no one even notices you when you first walk through the door. That's the most important moment of any occasion—the grand entrance. So, as I was saying, I came in, and you could almost hear the crowd inhale. I was that hot.

All night, John Keeler tried to pretend that he didn't even notice me. He isn't fooling me, though. He was with Pageboy Sage. He made a big production, talking to her and laughing out on the dance floor, but I caught him staring at me on at least four different occasions. I can just imagine how he's eating his heart out over how great I looked compared to Sage in her one-size-fits-all corduroy jumper or whatever dorky thing she had on. To be honest, I didn't even notice what she was wearing. It was probably too drab for words.

Only one guy asked me to dance. Momma says it's because I'm so beautiful that most boys are afraid to approach me. But that didn't stop that horrible Brandon McCormick. AS IF! I wouldn't be caught dead dancing with that stooge if he were the last guy on earth. He's rude and annoying. He came to the dance dressed like our band director, Mr. Dicky. Mr. Dicky wears outlandish clothes: baggy pants, sandals, and striped pullover shirts. I suppose Brandon thought he was being funny, or maybe that's all he had in his wardrobe. He's dirt poor.

As I was saying, Brandon walked right up to me and said, "Come on, Sky, looks like *you've* got plenty of room on your dance card." I told him, "In your dreams, moron!" He laughed just like the baboon that he is then ambled off to harass someone else.

I was already peeved about that jerk Brandon having the nerve to ask me, Sky Davis, to dance, when Courtney up and broke one of our rules. She danced with a guy who wasn't on our list. Well, it wasn't exactly a rule.

Officially, we're only forbidden to *go out* with boys who aren't on the list. All the same, Courtney knew from the look I gave her that she shouldn't say yes. But she went ahead and did it! In my opinion, she deserves to be banned from the group for at least a week. She has to learn that whenever one of us does something to embarrass ourselves, it embarrasses all of us. Dancing with a nobody makes all of us look bad.

Other than the Brandon thing and Courtney's faux pas, the evening went well, I think. John *was* looking at me, and I was by far the best dressed. I left everyone with a great impression. What more can a girl ask for at her first school dance?

Tuesday
September 3
Sage

John and I went to the school dance together even though we're not boyfriend/girlfriend anymore. We tried that this summer. It didn't work out. I'm not really interested in all that stuff yet. Maybe it's because I'm sort of a tomboy or because I get so sick of my mother constantly talking about men, or maybe it's Dad's obsession with Carly. I don't know. The whole dating thing sort of makes me sick.

But John is still my best friend. He's funny, and he likes to talk about interesting things. He's really cute, but that isn't what I like best about him. I guess what I like about him most is that he's always honest. He understands things too—like how embarrassed I get by my mother.

John likes Joanne De Leon. He told me at the dance. I noticed him looking at her while we were dancing, but I didn't say anything. I knew he'd tell me about it later, and he did. I suppose I should be jealous in some way, but I'm not. Like I said, I'm not into all of that stuff, and if John likes Joanne, it's okay by me. John never asked her to dance. Maybe because he wasn't sure how I'd take it. Or it may have been because Joanne was standing next to Sky most of the night.

John avoids Sky Davis because she's the most hateful girl at Prescott. He used to be her boyfriend until he got sick of her bossing him around and ended it. She went nuts when he told her that he didn't want to go out with her anymore. She told him that he wasn't anything but a "bookworm from a middle-class family." She even insulted the car his parents drove. John doesn't want to provoke Sky. She'll make a scene at the drop of a hat, just to be the center of attention. She's been like that ever since I've known her, which is pretty much since kindergarten. Once in first grade, she threw a fit because someone else was using the red crayon and she wanted it. She stamped her foot, cried, and when that didn't work, held her breath until she started to turn blue. Finally, the kid handed her the crayon. That's the way it's always been with Sky. She'll do anything to get her way.

Thursday
September 5
Joanne

It's been five days since the dance, and that is still all Sky is talking about. I think that if she asks me one more time if I saw John Keeler looking at her or how much I liked her dress, I will just vomit. Really, I don't know if John Keeler was looking at her or not. I wasn't paying all that much attention. But I reassure her that he was, and go on and on about her lovely dress and her gorgeous ringlets hoping that someday we can get off this and onto another topic.

I didn't enjoy the dance at all. First of all, none of us danced except Courtney. That's because there are only three guys on our "approved list." One of them wasn't there, the other had a date, and the third is John Keeler, who danced with Sage all night. Last week, there were six boys on "the list," but three of them were dropped for wearing last year's clothes to school this year. It's incredible how Sky can keep a mental catalog of everyone's wardrobe. She'll walk by someone at school and say, "For God's sake, doesn't that girl have any clothes? She wore that exact same outfit just last Wednesday."

Poor Courtney made the mistake of dancing with a boy that had been X'd off the list for wardrobe violation. He wore a brand of jeans that Sky said went out of style two years ago. We've been forbidden to speak to Courtney until Friday, which is tomorrow, thank God. I can't stand to see her eating alone for one more day. I don't think the others like Sky's rules any more than I do. But we don't argue. Sky can be terribly vindictive. No one wants to be the one to speak out because we can only imagine what she'll do to get even.

I tried to talk to Tiffany at the dance. She looked through me as if I didn't exist and then turned her back and pretended to be busy. I don't blame her for ignoring me. Why should she want to have anything to do with me after I burned her the last time? I don't know why I even bother. I couldn't hang out with her again even if she did forgive me because Sky would never approve. But I want Tiffany to tell me that it's okay, that she's over it and it was no big deal. I suppose I'm just trying to ease my own conscience.

Monday
September 9
Sky

I am miffed beyond words. Today in Spanish class, I just happened to notice that Joanne was reading a note. When I leaned across the aisle to ask who it was from, she tried to stick it in her notebook. I snatched it out of her hand. We don't keep secrets in our group. That's a rule—at least it is now. It was from John Keeler, of all people. Can you believe it? He's using my best friend to try to make me jealous!

It won't work. John knew I'd see that note. It's all part of his game to try to win me back. He said all sorts of weak stuff to her about how he'd like to have her over sometime to watch a movie. Poor Joanne. I hope she doesn't think he's serious. What he's doing is just awful. The very idea! I'll show him. If he thinks I'm going to let him get to me, he has another think coming. I'm going to play along as if it doesn't bother me one bit—because of course, it doesn't. Momma says that men will do anything to get a woman's attention, but this is just too pathetic.

I hope that this is the first letter John's written to poor Joanne. She assured me that it was. I'm sure she's telling the truth since she didn't mention any letters this weekend when she and the others slept over at my house. It certainly would have come up, too, since they were all telling me how John couldn't keep his eyes off me last weekend at the dance. Joanne should know that he's just trying to use her in his little game. For God's sake! *Joanne*? For one thing, she doesn't even have what I'd call a body. She's as thin as a rail and as flat-chested as a fourth grader. Besides, I don't even think that John's dad would approve. You know, the whole interracial dating thing doesn't go over with most parents.

Tuesday
September 10
Sage

Mom has a new boyfriend. His name is Russell. We bumped into him last weekend at the Mini Mart. He was wearing coveralls with a name tag sewed above the pocket and "White Knight Plumbing Service" in big, bold letters on the back. He and Mom made eye contact as he turned away from the register with his purchase of a six-pack of beer and a carton of cigarettes. Then on Monday, our toilet suddenly stopped up. What a coincidence. Mom just happened to remember the number of Russell's company and gave him a call—a damsel in distress. For only 35 bucks, her toilet was freed of the washcloth that "someone" had "accidentally" flushed, and she got a date.

Mom really likes him. But, then again, she's *really* liked every guy she's gone out with. All of her relationships end pretty much the same. At first, everything will go along just fine. Then after about a whole three weeks, Mom starts pushing for some kind of commitment, and *wham bam*, her boyfriend is out the door like a scalded cat. Well, maybe not all that fast. Some of them try to be decent about it. They simply stop calling as often or start making excuses why they can't come over.

It's really a blessing in disguise. Every boyfriend has been weirder than the last. There was the disc jockey who wore purple spandex pants and had a ponytail; the football coach who thought he was God's gift to women (even though his glory days were all the way back in high school when he had hair and could still see past his belly to tie his shoes); and the ancient guy with the sports car, gold chains, and shirt unbuttoned to his navel. There have been others too numerous and ridiculous to count. The point is, they're all losers, and they aren't good enough for my mom.

Mom doesn't see it that way, though. She takes each new rejection harder than the last. Every time she gets dumped, Brandy and I have to slink around the house for several days so we don't set her off. She's angry when she's hurt. Sometimes she says things that I know she doesn't mean. Like the last time a guy broke up with her, she told us, "Men just don't want women who have a bunch of extra baggage." She meant us. We used to be her girls; now we're "baggage."

Mom isn't really mean, though. She's just been crazy since Dad left. I don't know her anymore. Sometimes, when she has her hopes up over some new guy, she gets happy again and cleans the house, cooks great meals, and plays games with us like she used to. Then she gets hurt and falls back into a depression. Maybe things will be different with Russell. I think he's a slob, and I don't really want a stepdad, but if that's what it would take to make Mom the way she used to be, I suppose I could learn to live with it.

Wednesday
September 11
Joanne

Friday night, Sky had the whole gang over to spend the night. Courtney had already done penance for the crime of dancing with a "nobody." Her sentence of being shunned had officially ended at 4:00 that day. It wasn't really over, though. Once someone does something to thwart Sky's authority, she's not one to let it go easily. She made a point of either criticizing Courtney or openly ignoring her the entire evening. Courtney just smiled and took it, as is our custom. What was she supposed to do? Say something to Sky in her own house and risk being asked to leave? That's actually happened before. Last year, Sky made some nasty comment to Julia, so Julia made a cut back at her. Sky marched over to the door, threw it open, and told Julia to "get out of her house." Julia had to beg to use the phone so she could get a ride home. Sky wanted to put her out on the street right then and there. It was terribly embarrassing for everyone.

The night started out awkward, and it didn't get any better. Sky put on the dress she had worn to the dance and paraded around the room for all of us to admire one more time. Her mother came in and oooohhhhed and aaaaaahhhhed until I thought I was going to be ill. I don't know what is happening to me. Am I just overly critical all of a sudden, or have things always been this ridiculous? We spent at least two hours rehashing Sky's performance at the dance: how she stood, how she looked, how she snubbed John Keeler.

Then things got even worse. Sky's mom broke out with home movies starring the one and only, you guessed it—Sky. We watched her dance recitals, birthday parties, Christmas pageants, and every other production she'd been in from the time she could walk across a stage. It was the most tedious evening of my entire life! I even thought about pretending to be sick so that I could go home. It wouldn't have taken all of that much pretending either. I honestly felt nauseous.

The next morning, we all went out on the lawn to practice our routines for cheerleading tryouts, which are Friday. This will be the first year that we can try out. The sixth grade just has a pep squad. Anyone can be in that. Members just have to buy the outfit and keep their grades up. Seventh grade gets to have a real cheer squad. We try out in front of the whole student body, and they have a popular vote. There will be six girls chosen out of about 25. We're all fairly sure that we'll be on the squad. We went to cheerleading camp this summer, and we're pretty good. Also, the most popular girls are usually the ones to make it. That's the way cheerleading has always been.

Sky is positive that she'll receive the most votes and therefore be elected head cheerleader. She's counted on this since the first day of the first grade. We debated about who we thought would be the sixth girl. Several other girls from Prescott went to camp too. But each of them, according to Sky, has some strike against her: not popular, too fat, not pretty. I actually pity the poor girl who does win the spot. She'll be under Sky's command with the rest of us, and I guarantee Sky will let her know she doesn't belong.

I'm really mad at Sky right now. Only she doesn't know it because, as usual, I didn't have the guts to tell her off when she grabbed John's note out of my hand in Spanish class Monday. I can't believe her sometimes! She has the manners of a billy goat. To make matters worse, after she read it, she didn't even get mad. I mean, you'd think she'd be jealous. But not Sky. Instead, she looked at me like I was being taken in by some big hoax. Of course, she wouldn't believe that a boy would prefer me over her. She's just so arrogant.

THURSDAY
SEPTEMBER 12
BRANDON

Do I have a plan! I figured out how to kill two birds with one stone. So far this year, there are three people on my list: The Tank, Sky Davis, and my stepdad. I still haven't come up with a way to mow down The Tank. But I got one comin' for Sky and Pop.

I hate Sky 'cause she's a snotty little brat with a bad attitude, and I hate Pop 'cause he thinks he can move in and run my life. Last week, The Tank called him to "discuss my behavior." She was all bent 'cause I saluted her and yelled, "SIR YES SIR" when she told me to open my book. She didn't think it was all that funny. She told Pop that I'd disrespected her, and she acted like maybe my upbringing had been questionable or something. He was ticked! He said I was an embarrassment to the family and all that crap. Then he told me that he and Mom have talked it over and decided I should get into sports or some other "extracurricular activity" at school. He said I had too much spare time on my hands to get into trouble. He started going off about how he had played football when he was a kid and that being in athletics gives you discipline and blah, blah, blah.

Now, here's the thing about Pop. Once you get in something, you can't ever quit. When I was eight, I thought I wanted to be in gymnastics 'cause my cousin Greg was in it. Mom signed me up and drove Greg and me the 30 miles to the city every Tuesday. Then on Thursdays, Aunt Kelly drove us. After about three weeks, I was sick of the whole thing. It all seemed pretty stupid to me, and the instructors at the school worked us 'til I could barely stand it. I told Mom that I wanted out. She was gonna let me quit, too, but *oh no*! She'd just started datin' old Pop, and he told her that it'd build character to make me "stick to my commitments." He told her even though gymnastics was for "girls and pretty boys," I'd wanted to join, and by God, I'd stick it out. I had to hang with that torture for three years 'til Mom finally decided to let me quit on account of my cousin had quit two years earlier, she was sick of drivin' 120 miles a week, and we couldn't afford it anymore.

Well, do I have a surprise for Pop. All of that "sticking to my commitment" is finally gonna pay off, but not by "improving my character" like he had wanted. He thought I had embarrassed the family before, but just wait 'til he sees what I'm gonna do next. I'll give him somethin' to brag about with his old army buddies down at the VFW. Like a dutiful son, I've chosen my "extracurricular" activity, and it's gonna be a blast. I can get a lick in on Pop, bring Sky down off her high horse, and get an eyeful of leg, all at the same time.

Friday
September 13
Tiffany

This week was one exciting moment after another. I sit back and watch all of the soap operas unfold before my eyes and thank God

I'm not part of any of them. There's safety in silence.

We all assembled in the gym after lunch to watch the parade of fools as they tried out for the ever-coveted title of "cheerleader." Why anyone would want to get up in front of hundreds of people and jump around in short skirts and yell idiotic ditties is beyond me.

Anyway, everything went as predicted for the first 30 minutes. Miss Laughinghouse, who's been saddled with the job of cheerleading sponsor, got up in front of the student body and made a speech about team spirit, hard work, rewarding talent, blah, blah, blah. She instructed everyone to "put popularity and friendship aside and vote for the girls who are most talented."

Tryouts began. Everyone's routine was pretty much the same. They came out jumping around, doing cartwheels, yelling "Two bits, three bits . . ." or "Give me a P . . ." Then they ended the whole thing with the splits or a high kick and ran off the floor to giggle in dread and drill their buddies about their performance.

Then came Sky Davis. I have no idea where she found a blue sequined costume just for tryouts, but there she was, sporting the latest fashion in cheerleading attire, flipping her hair around and yelling at the top of her lungs, "Apple pie, banana split, we think your team plays like shhhh—ake it to the left, shake it to the right."

I got a look at Principal Williams just as all the color drained from his face. I wasn't sure what shocked him more, the way Sky turned around and "shook it" for the audience, or her allusion to profanity. Anyway, I thought it was over when out came one last candidate . . . Brandon McCormick!

Man, you should have seen him go! He did about five back flips, went into a somersault, and ended in the splits, which looked absolutely, anatomically impossible (given the fact that he's a boy and all). The crowd went wild. No one had expected a boy to go out for cheerleading. I don't think that's ever happened in the history of this school. And he was good too. He made the girls look like a bunch of one-legged men in a kicking contest.

We all voted and went back to class. I happen to have Sky Davis in my eighth period, so I was there to watch the ax fall. Miss Laughinghouse came over the intercom and gave a pep talk full of worn-out clichés like "It's not whether you win or lose, etc., etc." Sky looked like she'd bust a gut by the time Laughinghouse got around to announcing the winners. She started out by saying who was in: Courtney, Sky, Joanne, Julia, Candice—and then she dropped the bomb. "Our head cheerleader, the one who received the most votes, is Brandon McCormick." Ha! Who would have thought? I'd have given my eyeteeth to have caught Sky's face on film. She looked just like this big catfish my dad brought home from the lake last week. Her mouth opened and closed about three times, and her throat was working like she had to struggle to draw breath.

I couldn't help but stare at her. It isn't every day you get to see Sky Davis lose. She shoved her books off her desk, jumped up, and ran out of the room. On her way to the door, she tried to share her humiliation with me by yelling in my face, "What are you looking at, *freak*?" Everyone burst out laughing. I thought I was going to die of embarrassment until I realized that they weren't even laughing at me. They were laughing at Sky.

That was when I figured out that Sky's popularity has always been nothing more than our bad habit. We'd all gotten so used to letting her be first that we'd forgotten we had a choice. Ever since first grade, she's bullied her way to the front of the line, so totally convinced that she was entitled, that we were all convinced as well. Now the tables have turned. It was as if the wicked princess's reign of terror had come to an end and every faction of her kingdom was united in one big laughing sigh of relief.

Monday
September 16
Sky

Prescott Junior High School has gone completely *whack*! It's like I went to sleep one night and everything was normal, then the next day I'd been transported into the Twilight Zone. I was shocked beyond words that Brandon McCormick—idiot boy—was elected as the head cheerleader of the seventh grade. *He isn't even popular!* I really think there is more to this than meets the eye. When that sappy, do-gooder, Miss Laughinghouse, made the announcement, I marched straight out of my eighth period class and up to the office to demand a recount. They wouldn't even give me that. The hick secretary told me that the vote hadn't even been *close*! She said, "Why, Sky Daaarlin', Brandon won head cheerleader by a laaandslide." I don't believe it. Someone is on the take.

To make matters worse, my very own friends, who should have been sympathetic to my pain, had a swim party at Courtney's on Saturday and invited *him*! Courtney didn't even act sorry. She told me that we'd planned the party for the cheer squad weeks before the election, and that meant that whoever was elected was supposed to come. She used practice as an excuse to include that baboon. I know that we only have one week before the first football game, but all the same, you would think that my friends would have the decency not to rub my nose in defeat the very day after I suffered such agony.

Oh, I'm just furious! I could bite the head off a live chicken! You should have seen Brandon, sunning himself by the pool in his baggy Tasmanian Devil swim trunks, sipping a

Coke float through a straw like he was the king of Egypt or something. He had on mirrored sunglasses, for God's sake. I couldn't even tell what the pervert was looking at. I can only imagine! He had the nerve to shake his empty glass at me when I walked by. He said, "Sky, baby, do ya mind? I'm a little dry here." Oh, I was crazy mad. The others actually thought he was funny, showing off on the diving board, imitating teachers, telling stupid truck stop jokes.

Then when it was time for us to start practicing, he all of a sudden became Mr. Big-Shot. I had a whole routine all planned for Friday's game, and he just jumped in and changed everything. My so-called "friends" were begging him to teach them some of his gymnastic tricks. The attention went straight to his head, I'll tell you. I couldn't take another minute. I called Momma and told her to come get me. I'll have no part of this. Come Friday, when it's time to get out in front of the crowd, we'll see who runs this show.

Tuesday
September 17
Joanne

How things can change in one short week. Just when I was completely bored with everything around me, the world went from black-and-white to full-blown Kodak color. I made the cheerleading team, as did all of my friends and Brandon McCormick.

We had a victory party at Courtney's. Courtney invited Brandon even though she knew Sky would probably make a scene. I don't know how Courtney found the courage to stand up to Sky the way she did. She simply told her—no ifs, ands, or buts—that the party was for the whole squad, and Brandon was not only part of the squad but the lead. I think Courtney was still sore over the way Sky treated her at the sleepover. You could tell by the look on Courtney's face when Sky faced her off and demanded that Brandon be excluded, she had finally had enough. It was great!

We had a blast at the pool party. At first, we didn't even think that Sky would show up, but she came about 30 minutes late, as usual.

She was wearing a thong bikini, if you can believe it. Courtney's mom just about choked on her hot dog when Sky came waltzing through the gate practically naked. As soon as Sky got there, everyone became tense. We all knew that she was mad as a hornet, but she played it off like she wasn't a bit bothered. That is until Brandon asked her to get him another Coke. I'll admit that Brandon was picking on Sky. You could see how much he was enjoying his victory. She took his glass to the bar and fixed him another float. Then she walked over and dumped it right in the crotch of his swim trunks.

I do feel a little sorry for Sky. She'd always been positive that she'd be the leader of our cheer squad, and now here's this boy calling all the shots. He's fantastic though. If we can learn what Brandon knows, we could be an even better squad than they have at the high school. He's big enough to lift us and form a base for pyramids. He can also do terrific flips and handsprings. We were trying to learn some of them when Sky just up and left. None of us even noticed that she'd gone until later.

We felt bad for her, but the party sure picked up. We gave Brandon a manicure, and he even let us paint his toenails. We were all pretty sick of our own company, so Brandon coming along was like a breath of fresh air. I've always thought that Brandon was a complete dolt. He acts silly all the time. You wouldn't think he had a brain in his head. But he really does. He's actually witty sometimes. He's not the kind of guy that I'd be interested in dating or anything. If my grandmother met Brandon she would say, "*Le patina el coco.*" That means that his coconut slips, or in English, "he has a screw loose." He's as weird as they come. But weird in a fun way. He's just different, that's all.

Wednesday
September 18
Sage

Brandy and I went hiking out at the state nature area with Dad and Carly last weekend. It was fun, especially for Brandy, who's always finding new things for her collection. She has everything from old marbles to paper clips in a box under our bed. Every once in a while, she takes them all out and tells me where each and every thing came from. She found an old cow's tooth on the trail this weekend, and she's convinced it's a fossil from the ice age.

Dad and Carly are talking about getting married. I suppose they may as well, since she practically lives with him anyway. I wonder how Mom will take it. I'm always trying to figure out what Carly sees in my dad. He's way older than she is, he's going bald, and he isn't rich. I just don't get it. You'd think she'd want someone that didn't already have kids and a lifetime subscription to *Reader's Digest*. But she hangs on him like he's the hottest thing going. Go figure!

Mom and Russell are still going strong. Of course, it's only been a week, so I'm not making rice bags or sewing beads on her wedding slippers just yet. He came over last night and watched television with us. Mom jumped up and down off the couch every ten minutes to bring him a beer or get him a snack. Russell sat there like Jabba the Hut, sucking down one beer after another, dropping crumbs onto our sofa, and flipping through channels with the remote. He didn't even stop for a second to ask what anyone else wanted to watch. Then Mom sent us to bed at 8:00. We don't ever go to bed that early. I suppose that she thought "the baggage" might get in the way of romance with the pot-bellied plumber.

Friday night is the first football game of the season. John and I are going, and we're taking Brandy along because Mom and Russell have a date. I'm really not all that crazy about football, but it beats sitting at home. Besides, I want to see our new cheer squad in action. I'm sure John does too, but for different reasons. He's still hung up on Joanne, even though she hasn't said "Boo" to him since he wrote her that note. I'm going to watch the power struggle between Sky and Brandon. I still feel like cracking up when I think that Brandon McCormick managed to pull the lead position right out from under Sky Davis. She's such a spoiled brat.

Brandon's strange. I've never been friends with him or even spoken to him that I can think of, but I've gone to school with him ever since I can remember. Come to think of it, I've never known Brandon to have any real friends. Everyone knows him, and the guys all think he's hilarious, but I've never noticed that he hung around with any one crowd. He just drifts. His clothes are always a little wrinkled like he just pulled them out of the laundry basket, and he doesn't spend a lot of time on his hair either. He just doesn't seem to care much what people think. He can be terribly annoying when he's acting like a fool in class, but you have to admire his guts. How many guys would go out for cheerleading knowing that they'll be made fun of by every jock on campus?

Thursday
September 19
Tiffany

I never thought I'd be in a position to feel sorry for Brandon McCormick. He's the silliest kid I've ever seen. To tell you the truth, I totally hated him for the longest time. When we were in the third grade, my sister gave me a puppet for Christmas. She'd made it from a kit she bought at the craft store. It was a purple dragon with big bulging eyes. I loved that puppet. I took it to school one day for show and tell. Brandon grabbed it off my desk and started running around the room sticking it in kids' faces and making belching noises.

Some girl tried to take it from him. When he yanked it away, its whole nose tore off. I cried for hours.

I don't know what to think of Brandon now. He made Sky look stupid, which could almost make him my hero if I hadn't already despised him. Now, he's catching it from a lot of the jocks on the football team. They call him names that I'd be embarrassed to write. Most of the guys are doing it to impress Sky. She has a whole new following now. It seems like things are starting to fall apart with her old crowd, so the girls who always wanted to be her friends and didn't rate are sucking up in hope that they'll have a chance. The guys that are ribbing Brandon probably see this as an opportunity to hit on Sky while she's down and out. They like her because of her body. Her personality is the pits, but boy does she have a figure!

Anyway, Brandon doesn't seem to mind the negative attention. Someone wrote a bad name with a permanent marker in big black letters on his locker. He took a black marker and added letters so it read:

FANTASTIC
P.H.A.T.
GRECIAN
GOD
OF
PRESCOTT

Monday
September 23
Sky

I have had it! The cheer squad got together at the football field after school on Friday to practice a little before the game. Brandon called everyone into a huddle and announced that we were going to have rules for our squad "to make everything fair and on the 'up and up.' " Here are the rules:

1. *We all wear regulation uniforms—no deviations.*

   He said this was because it wouldn't be fair to everyone else on the squad if one person showed up in a "tiara and a brocade gown" just to draw attention away from the others and onto him or herself. I think it's because he's too poor to afford any nice clothes, and this way, he can make sure no one outdoes him.

2. *We perform the routines that we've all agreed to before the games.*

Brandon said, "That way, no one will argue and make a scene in the middle of the game when we are supposed to be doing our cheers." It's really because he's on a power trip and he doesn't want to try anyone's ideas but his own.

3. *All pyramids or stunts requiring that we "build upward" have to be done on the soft track on the edge of the field.*

   Duh! So no one will get hurt—obviously.

4. *Insubordination to the squad leader will be cause for suspension.*

   "After all, we are a team," said Brandon. Really! The nerve of him. What a tyrant!

5. *Anyone who misses a practice will be mascot for the following game!*

   He said this was "incentive for us to come to practice, because if someone doesn't practice the routine, he or she will throw the

> others off." But what he's really doing is punishing me for me for walking out of Courtney's pool party last Saturday.

I was so furious that I just let him have it. I told him that I wasn't taking orders from a trailer-trash drag queen. He said, "Please refer to rule number four." *Oh!* I am going to get even with Brandon McCormick if it's the last thing I do!

Monday
September 23
Sage

John, Brandy, and I went to the game Friday night. Unfortunately, so did Mom and Russell. That was her big date—greasy chili dogs and a reserved seat at Prescott Junior High's football game. I didn't even know Mom was there until the end of the first quarter. When I heard her voice screaming, "Go, Prescott, Go!" I thought it was just some really loud woman that sounded like Mom. But there she was, in bright green skin-tight capri pants and a flowered halter top, standing in the front row of section H. Russell was sitting down wedging a chili dog into his face as if he hadn't had a bite to eat since Christmas dinner.

I don't want people to see my mom the way she is now. She looks so desperate. She's really pretty when she's just being herself, without all the makeup, skimpy clothes, and pretending. For God's sake, she doesn't even like football, and there she was hooting and hollering like it was her favorite sport in the whole world just to impress a slug like Russell. I felt my face go hot. John noticed. He tousled my hair and smiled at me to let me know it was all okay. I relaxed a little. After all, there was no reason to get embarrassed. She was way over in section H, and we were in section E. Then Brandy stood up and yelled, "Hey, Mommy!" Of course, Mom couldn't hear her over the crowd, but no fewer than ten people looked from Brandy to Mom and made the connection. I saw a couple of them elbow each other and snicker.

We went back to watching the game. I was trying to figure out where Sky had disappeared to. All of the cheerleaders were on the sidelines doing acrobatics and shouting slogans to the crowd, but Sky wasn't with them. Even if she'd come down with the plague, she wouldn't miss an opportunity to grandstand in front of an audience. Maybe she was just being "fashionably late" and at any minute would come prancing onto the field riding a white stallion and twirling flaming batons.

I was pondering the possibilities when Brandy started shouting about the "big pussycat." Our team is the Prescott Panthers. Because, of course, we can't have a real panther for a mascot, we have this ancient costume that someone made back when the school first opened. It has a huge, round head made of chicken wire and covered with black velvet. One ear is shredded, and there are only about two whiskers left on each side of the nose, which by the way, is a triangle of fake leather that someone painted pink. The body of the costume is huge. The crotch sags so low that it looks like Kitty had an accident and needs a change. The feet are made of diving flippers built up with Styrofoam balls and covered with the same worn-out velvet. The hands aren't homemade. Someone bought them later from a costume store. Except the palms are white instead of solid black like the rest of the outfit, so they look out of place. Ours is the ugliest, most pathetic mascot costume in the entire county. It doesn't look like a panther at all, but an old stuffed alley cat that someone's grandmother made out of discarded black socks and other household castoffs.

The "big pussycat" paced around out on the field for a while. Then at half-time, Brandon whispered something in its shredded ear, and it came up into the stands to pass out little plastic footballs to the kids. Brandy was screaming for one, so John hollered at the cat to come over our way. I could have sworn that pussycat was ignoring us on purpose. We ended up having to get up and walk five bleachers down to get Brandy her ball.

That's when I figured out where Sky had been. When Brandy grabbed her ball, I noticed Sky's charm bracelet peeking out from beneath "the big kitty's" velvet sleeve. I couldn't help but smile. It was just too funny. Sky caught my look. She turned around and stomped off toward the field—her crooked coat hanger tail sticking out like an exclamation point.

Wednesday
September 25
Tiffany

I sat with Mom and Dad at the game on Friday—of course. All of the other kids sit together in section E. That's the section at the end. Most of them don't really watch the game. They hang over the fence on the edge of the bleachers and yell at people or throw ice on their heads as they walk by.

We sat near Brandon's parents. I wouldn't have even known they were his parents if I hadn't been listening to their conversation—well, argument, really. Until then, I'd never thought of Brandon as having parents. I thought he'd been hatched in the desert by vultures or something. Anyway, they were arguing about Brandon. His mom seemed kind of excited about his performance. She said something about his skill in gymnastics, and then his dad got this disgusted look on his face and started ranting about how Brandon was an embarrassment to the family. He used some of the names I'd heard the jocks calling Brandon lately. Brandon's mom looked like she wanted to hit him, but instead she got up and mumbled some excuse about going to get peanuts.

Brandon's dad is a jerk. I can't believe he'd call his son names like that. Sure, most dads wouldn't be crazy about their son being a cheerleader, but Brandon really is good at it, and that should count for something. His dad is one of those big hulking guys who looks like he played football in college. I suppose he'd wanted Brandon to follow in his footsteps and be a tough guy. I'm sure cartwheels on the sidelines weren't part of his plan. No wonder Brandon doesn't get ruffled when the jocks hassle him at school. He probably gets it worse at home.

The game drew a big crowd because it was the first game of the season. That probably made it worse for Sky. It must have been embarrassing traipsing around in that big, musty cat costume all night. No one would have known it was her if Brandon hadn't made an announcement at half-time. He used his megaphone to introduce himself and the other cheerleaders. Then he requested special applause for "The Prescott Panther." He pulled the mascot over next to him and removed the big chicken-wire head. There was Sky—her hair plastered to her face with sweat, looking as if she were about to cry. I almost felt sad for her.

THURSDAY
SEPTEMBER 26
BRANDON

My "extracurricular activity" is panning out even better than I'd hoped. Pop flipped when I told him and Mom I was on the cheer squad. He threw his magazine on the floor and went to the kitchen for another beer. Not a word, but his face said enough. Mom was nice about it. Only, she looked at me kinda weird, like she wasn't sure if I'd lost my mind or somethin'. They came to the game on Friday. I heard them fightin' about it for hours Thursday night. Mom was telling Pop that "we should be supportive." Pop asked her if she was gonna "be supportive" when I started "wearin' pantyhose and lipstick." Ha! Instead of bein' Pop's jock, I'm more like his jock itch. He digs at me like nobody's business at home, callin' me "sweetheart" and "little girl." But if he scratches me in public, everyone will see him for the big stupid jerk he is!

I've got the brat over a barrel. Sky draggin' around in that cat costume would have been enough to make the whole cheer squad gig worthwhile all by itself. But it gets even better than that. The other girls are great. I think they're really gettin' a kick out of the whole thing. Sky had 'em all scared to go to the toilet without her permission. Now she's not in control, at least not in the cheer squad, and they're all kickin' it up—waitin' on me hand and foot, goin' along with all my ideas like I'm king _____. A regular harem.

This is gonna be a great year. I got beautiful chicks jumpin' around me in miniskirts and havin' me over for swim parties at their million-dollar shacks. I'm on my way to fulfillin' my life's ambition. Brandon McCormick—The Next American Gigolo.

chapter 3

October

Timid One

Head down

Upside-down reader

Minority leader?

All Hallow's Eve

Unknown guest

Beautiful dancer?

Venture a guess.

Joshua

Tuesday
October 1
Joanne

This past Friday, our team played against the Owls at their field in Varley, which is about 60 miles away. The cheer squad rode on a school bus with the football players. It was fun, even though Sky was in a nasty mood and tried to start trouble.

We all sat together on the ride there. Brandon sat between Julia and Courtney in the backseat, while Sky, Candice, and I took the seat right in front of them. Brandon was all kicked back with an arm around each girl, headphones in his ears, chanting lyrics, and munching on a huge supply of snacks he'd brought along for the ride.

Sky kept turning around in the seat to tell him to "Shut up," but he ignored her like he couldn't hear over the music. Then she said as loudly as she could, "You'd think the government would put limits on what people can buy with food stamps" while throwing a disapproving glance at Brandon's bag of food. She said, "Daddy says that there are a lot of people living on disability who aren't even sick. They're just lazy and want us to support them." It was obvious that she was directing all of this at Brandon, but he just went on munching and singing like he couldn't hear a word she said.

Sky got so put out, she jumped up and pushed her way to the front of the bus to tell the driver that Brandon was "listening to vulgar music on a CD player, which, by the way, is against school rules." The bus driver didn't seem all that concerned, but she harped on about how her daddy is an attorney and that Brandon's singing offensive lyrics could be considered sexual harassment. Finally, the driver yelled back for Brandon to put the CD player away. Sky pranced back to our seat, just as pleased as if she'd won a major court battle all by herself.

The game went okay, even though we lost. Since no one had missed practice this week, Brandon volunteered to be the mascot. He really hammed it up. He chased the Varley Owl along the sidelines pretending to claw him, got on all fours and arched his back like an angry cat, danced, and did flips. The crowds on both sides were in stitches.

On the trip home, Sky told Brandon off about "stealing the show." She said that he was always trying to get attention for himself and it wasn't fair to the rest of the team. She tried to get us all to agree that Brandon had been wrong, but the rest of us really didn't care all that much. That made her even angrier, so she went and sat with the quarterback. For the rest of the ride home, they whispered to each other, looked at Brandon, and cackled like chickens. This was supposed to hurt Brandon's feelings, I suppose, but he had fallen fast asleep with his head on Courtney's shoulder, as oblivious as a baby.

Wednesday
October 2
Sky

Momma got the scoop on Mr. Brandon Bossy-Butt McCormick. She asked around and found out all kinds of interesting information from her friends. Seems Brandon's stepdad is a loser. He's a veteran who supposedly has some sort of heart trouble, so he collects disability from the government. Also, one of Momma's friends saw Brandon's mother at the grocery store paying for her food with welfare. Food stamps, for God's sake! They live in a trailer park over on the other side of the tracks. According to Momma's friends, his real dad left when Brandon was in first grade, and now he's filthy rich, but he let Brandon's stepdad adopt Brandon so he wouldn't have to pay child support.

I should have known Brandon was from one of THOSE families. And to think, he's hanging out with us like he actually belongs. I suppose I'd better warn the others to hide the silver when he comes over for practice. There's no telling what valuables he could stuff down those baggy britches of his!

They probably won't even listen when I tell them what he's really all about. I've just about had it with my so-called "friends." Brandon has infected them all like some sort of parasite. Like Momma says, "If you lie down with dogs, you get up with fleas." They just don't have any standards anymore. Julia actually wore overalls to school last week. She said they were "comfortable." How gross! I can't believe her mother let her out of the house looking like Old MacDonald. Next thing you know, she'll be sucking on hayseed and hocking up loogies into a red bandanna! The whole world has gone *nuts*!

Friday
October 4
Sage

Our writing prompt for the week is: When I was little, I believed in ________________.

When I was little, I believed in Santa Claus, the Easter Bunny, the Tooth Fairy, and grown-ups. First, you find out that your parents lied to you about all the other stuff, and then you find out they lie all the time. Dad lied to Mom all those nights that he was supposedly "working late" and he was really out with Carly. Mom lied to us when she said that everything would be fine after the divorce. If you can't believe your own parents, who can you believe?

Dad and Carly are married! Just last week they had said they were only thinking about it. Now he calls and says that they went ahead and "tied the knot" at the courthouse on

Tuesday. Mom tried to act like she wasn't bothered, but then she went out and stayed gone past midnight. I don't know why I feel so sad. Carly and Dad have been together for two years. I knew this was coming. It just seems so final. I suppose that part of me still believed in fairy tales. I was holding on to some unspoken hope that Dad would change his mind, dump Carly, and come back home.

Sometimes, I find myself thinking about how things used to be when we were a real family. We had dinner at the table every night, went on family vacations, rented movies, and ate popcorn and Sour Patch Kids in front of the television. But whenever I start running off down Memory Lane, I have to stop myself and think of something else. When your parents get a divorce, all of those family memories that are supposed to make you feel good make you feel terrible instead.

I started a photo album when I was nine. I cut pictures into geometric shapes and put them on the pages with captions that read "Camping at the Lake" or "Christmas at Grandma's." When Dad left, I hid the album in my closet. I can't bring myself to throw it away. I also can't bear the thought of ever looking at it again. Our smiling faces just remind me of how it was all a big lie. We thought we'd be a family forever, and then one day Dad came home and told Mom it was over. That simple. The shutter had clicked for the final time on the happy little Mobley family.

All of the pictures in my head—past and future—had to change from that minute on. Graduation, first day of college, my wedding—I'd had an image in my mind of how my whole life was going to play out. I'd see myself doing all of those monumental things. And in my mental picture, Mom, Dad, and Brandy were always smiling at me from the crowd. Now what am I supposed to imagine? Dad with Carly, Mom with God-knows-who, and poor Brandy trying to decide where she should sit.

Monday
October 7
Tiffany

For the past month and a half, I've spent every weekday morning with Garfield shaking his finger at me from the poster in my corner, telling me "Apathy Is Not an Option." Maybe that's why I freaked out today in language arts class.

Poor old Jerky Josh left class to go to the bathroom. While he was gone, the kid that sits behind him took everything off of Josh's desk and hid it in a box under the overhead projector. When Josh came back, he stood there and stared at his empty desk like he was lost. Everyone started giggling, nudging neighbors, and pointing. Miss Laughinghouse didn't have a clue—as usual. She was up in front of the class talking about pronouns or prepositions while kids just milled around doing their own thing.

Anyway, it wasn't that big of a deal, I suppose. I'd seen kids do far worse things to Josh. But there was Garfield staring at me, and I simply couldn't take it anymore. I got up and walked to the overhead, got Josh's things, and put them back on his desk just the way he'd left them: pencils lined up, rubber bands and paper clips all in a neat row. Then I walked out. I didn't know where I was going. I just knew I had to get out of there. I ended up in the bathroom crying my eyes out. Not just over Josh, but everything. I'm sick of eating lunch by myself every day, sick of being ugly, and I'm really sick of mean people.

You would think that everyone who had ever been made fun of would remember how it felt the next time they thought about making fun of someone else. But they don't.

I'm an expert on how it feels. Next to Josh, I'm probably the second-most-made-fun-of kid at Prescott. Just like Josh, I'm an easy target. I don't normally fight back. Today I took a stand. I'm sure it'll buy me even more humiliation, but it felt good anyway.

I've been thinking a lot lately about how Joanne laughed at me that day when I passed by in the courtyard. I think that hurt more than anything anyone has ever said or done before, because deep down inside I know I've been guilty of doing the same thing. Joanne was just going along with everyone else because if she didn't, then she'd be the oddball. I do that too. I've sat in my desk, watched someone do something mean to someone else, and secretly been happy that it was the other person getting it this time instead of me. I mean, it's not like I openly make fun of anyone, but not doing anything to stop someone from hurting someone else, especially when you know how much it hurts, is just as bad.

I thought I really hated Joanne for being such a follower, but I suppose there's a little follower in everyone. I talked to Mom about it. We had one of those heart-to-hearts while I helped her peel potatoes for supper. She said that adolescents do that sort of thing because they want so badly to fit in. She said that as people get older, they're not as afraid to stand up and say what they think, even if it means other people won't like them. I don't know. Miss Laughinghouse lets kids do anything they want in class, like she's afraid we won't like her anymore if she gets tough and makes us do some work, and Principal Williams let Sky wear a cummerbund as a dress to the school dance because he's afraid to get on her parents' bad side. So some grown-ups are sellouts too, just like kids.

Tuesday
October 8
Sky

The lab rat has a crush on Jerky Josh! Yesterday in first period, she freaked out because some kid was picking on him. What a couple they'd make! Boy, can you imagine what their kids would be like? They're perfect for each other.

Look at me, wasting ink on a couple of weirdos when I could be writing about myself. Let's see, what should I write? I've been thinking about this week's writing prompt from Miss Laughinghouse: If I had a million dollars, I'd ____________________.

Of course, my parents already do have at least a million. But if I had a million to spend all by myself, I'd have a closet built onto my bedroom that would hold as many clothes as the outlet mall. Then I'd fly to Paris for a whole month. I'd shop at the finest stores, dine on *foie gras* at the *L'Ambroisie*, and let all of the best modeling agencies fight over me. I'd take Momma with me, of course, because she knows her way around Paris. She's been there twice, and she's practically a native, being that her great-grandmother was born in a little village on the Yonne.

I'd leave Daddy at home! He'd probably lecture me about how I spent my money. It seems like all he does these days is harp about bills. He's been following me around, turning off lights, and mumbling about wasting electricity. He even took Momma's MasterCard away from her. Can you believe it? He acts like we're poor or something!

As I was saying, Momma and I would stay in a luxurious hotel and meet all kinds of interesting people. I might even find me a handsome Parisian guy, and we could write long, romantic letters to each other after I returned to the States. When I got home, I'd quit school. After all, I already know everything I need to know for my career. I'm going to be a fashion model. What good will prepositional phrases do me when I'm waltzing down the runway in thousand-dollar dresses?

My modeling career would take right off, and I would travel the globe in high style. I'd have to find time to drop in on all of my old friends to show them how it is to live the high life, since lately they don't seem to have a clue.

Wednesday
October 9
Joanne

Grandmother Escamilla is here for a visit, and she brought my cousin Javier. I'm so happy to see them. I haven't seen Grandmother since this summer, and I haven't seen Javier since I was five. Until now, I'd only visited him once. He, my Uncle Joseph, and Aunt Teresa live in the mountainous region of Southern Mexico. The summer that we visited them was one of the best summers of my life. They have acres and acres of vineyards and an awesome house with covered balconies that look out onto a central courtyard. When I was there, Javier and I played hide-and-seek behind the fountains. I remember it as the most beautiful place I've ever seen.

The only problem with Grandmother's visit is that it came at a bad time. Tomorrow is my turn to have cheer squad practice at our house. When Mama told me that Grandmother was coming, I tried to get Julia or Courtney to have practice at one of their houses instead. Neither of them could. I didn't even ask Sky. She would have insisted on knowing why I didn't want to have it at my house, and I didn't have an excuse planned out.

I'm not ashamed of my grandmother. She is a beautiful lady. It's just that she doesn't speak English. I don't know how I'll talk to her in front of my friends without giving away my secret. God, how I wish I'd never pretended that I couldn't speak Spanish. So what? I'm bilingual. In this day and age, that's a definite plus on anyone's resumé. But since I've been sputtering over "uno, dos, tres" in Spanish class, they'll all see what a big liar I am if I start rattling off complete sentences to my relatives.

Oh well, I'll just hope for the best. Maybe Grandmother will stay in the house and there won't even be a problem. Javier speaks English just fine, but he speaks British English. He took English class at school, the same way we take Spanish as a foreign language class in the United States.

Friday
October 11
Sage

John and I sat with Tiffany Andrews at lunch today. I heard about what she'd done to stand up for Joshua Melton, and I got to thinking about how she's always alone. Every day at lunch, she eats by herself and then goes out into the courtyard to sit under a tree and read. I used to think that she just didn't like people very much, but then I started watching her. I noticed that she's always listening. I see her half smile when someone at the other end of the table cracks a joke, and when she's reading, she doesn't turn the pages. She's just been hiding behind her books to make people think she's off in her own world.

So today in the cafeteria, I took my tray and sat right across from her. John followed me and sat down with us. At first, Tiffany looked at us like we'd just landed there from outer space. Then she looked a little afraid, like we had some evil motive. Who could blame her for being suspicious? Kids at this school will do anything for a laugh, even sit next to someone unpopular and do something hideous like pretend to vomit in the poor kid's tray.

Once I sat down, I couldn't think of anything to say. We're both in Mrs. Clark's social studies class, so I tried to strike up a conversation by asking Tiffany what she thought of The Tank. She hesitated a minute and then said, "She's my favorite teacher." I thought she was kidding, but she didn't smile or laugh—just kept eating her peas.

I made a few more attempts to start a conversation, but I practically had to drag every word out of her. It was awkward. John chimed in with a comment once in while, and Tiffany would go beet-red. I don't think she's terribly comfortable around anyone, particularly guys. Then, after about 15 minutes, Tiffany picked up her book and her tray, excused herself, and went outside to "read."

I told John, "I think that went fairly well. Don't you?" He just tousled my hair and grinned.

Monday
October 14
Sky

Well, well, well! It was certainly an interesting weekend. We had a game on Friday. We lost again. Though to be honest, I didn't even know that until the next day. I was too busy cheering and thinking about the love of my life—Javier. He's Joanne's cousin, and he is absolutely gorgeous!

I went to Joanne's Thursday after school for practice. She hadn't even told me that her relatives were visiting. We were all there: Joanne, Courtney, Julia, Candice, and, of course, Brandon. I was right in the middle of a cheer, when HE walked out of the house. I swear I thought I'd died and gone straight to heaven. I just froze. He was wearing Dockers and a tight black T-shirt—Polo, I'm sure. He noticed me as soon as he came through the door. I could see it on his face—complete admiration. It was love at first sight, I tell you. Incredible! This beautiful foreign god has just dropped out of nowhere right into Joanne's backyard. I didn't even have to travel to Paris to find him. Oh, I am so excited!

He has dark, almond eyes, black hair, olive skin, and a body like a male model. He even speaks with a British accent. Well, I just quit practicing right then and there and started chatting with Javier about all kinds of interesting things. I told him all about myself. How I'm French and I'm going to be a model. I dropped hints about my parents' money. I didn't want to brag and appear vulgar, but I'm sure that a guy like Javier would only be interested in the crème de la crème. So I had to find subtle ways to let him know that I'm from a rich family. After all, with Brandon hanging around and Julia dressing like a farmhand, someone could easily think I was just another nobody. My "friends" aren't really helping my image these days.

As I was saying, Javier just sat and hung on every single word I said. Every once in a while he would look at Joanne and say something cute in Spanish. She'd just smile and giggle at him like she knew what he was saying. (I suppose she didn't want to hurt his feelings. I speak better Spanish than Joanne, and I can't even say my alphabet.) Of course, I didn't have any better idea than Joanne what Javier was saying, but I'll bet my life he was commenting on my lovely eyes or my long blonde hair.

The afternoon was going along like something out of a romance novel until Brandon had to step in and try to ruin things. He said I needed to get back to practice or I'd have to be the "kitty" at the game. It wasn't a total loss. Javier was watching us—well, me—the whole time, so I used practice as an opportunity to show him my assets. He was so impressed that at one point, he covered his face with his hands for several minutes. I think I saw that in a movie once. It's a foreign way of expressing complete awe. Kind of like saying, "You are so beautiful that I cannot bear to look!"

After the game on Friday, Momma asked Joanne and Javier if they wanted to go out to eat at El Flamenco. El Flamenco is a quaint little Spanish restaurant downtown. We all went except Daddy, who begged off to go home and check the electric meter, no doubt.

Momma read the menu just like Spanish was her second language. Javier raised his eyebrows at that! Momma can be quite impressive. I started telling Momma that Javier's family had vineyards back in Spain, when Joanne interrupted me. She said, "Mexico. They own vineyards in Mexico, Mrs. Davis." Same difference. I mean, it's not like

Javier lives in one of those ugly cardboard shacks on the border. I've been learning in Spanish class that there are actually a few people in Mexico who are incredibly wealthy. They're not like the Mexicans around here. Javier is from the Spaniard class of Mexico.

I actually have a fairly extensive knowledge of Mexico. Momma and I went shopping there once, and Mr. Silva has shown us several slide shows. So I tried to keep the conversation rolling. I asked Javier what he thought of the poverty in Mexico and how he could stand the sight of all those little beggars. He told me that every country has poverty. He said, "The United States is poor in ways that Mexico isn't." I asked him what he could possibly mean. We have everything here. After all, we are the richest country in the world. He said poverty and riches aren't always a matter of material things. Then he went into some story about a rich man whose relatives had to hire beggars from the street to cry at his funeral. I never really did catch what he meant. I think the story must have lost something in translation.

When we were about to leave the restaurant, Javier excused himself to go to the bathroom. I knew this would be my last chance to catch him alone, so I pretended that I needed to go as well. I caught him just before he went into the men's room. I didn't know how else to say it, we WERE pressed for time, so I asked him to kiss me right then and there. It was so sad, I tell you. He couldn't bring himself to take advantage of the moment. I meant more to him than a hasty kiss outside a bathroom door. He just put his hand on my face and said THE most romantic thing. He said, "Sky, you are what we call in Mexico *primada*." Then he went into the restroom. I'll always remember that moment—Javier touching my face and giving me the ultimate compliment in a foreign tongue. I just stared at that closing door with tears in my eyes. For me, the words *Cuarto de Baño los Hombres* will forever mean "Goodbye, my love."

Tuesday
October 15
Joanne

Poor Sky! She made such a fool of herself in front of my cousin. When we had practice at my house on Thursday, Sky went head-over-heels for Javier. As soon as she saw him, she started acting like an idiot. She sat at his feet on the deck chair and went on and on about her beautiful house, her mother's Mercedes, her father's position in his law firm. She even told him that she was going to Paris with her mother to interview with a modeling agency!

Javier thought she was the funniest thing on two legs. He'd sit and listen to her for a while, then turn to me and make a comment in Spanish. He said, "*Tus amiga ser mas listo que un coyote.*" That's a Mexican idiom that means something like "Your friend is as sharp as a tack." He was being sarcastic, of course. He thought Sky was as dull as mud. All day he would make sarcastic remarks about Sky to me and then turn back to listen to her as if he were really interested in every word she said. I couldn't help but laugh a little. Javier is so clever, and Sky is such an airhead. She honestly thought he was complimenting her in Spanish.

Just when I didn't think Sky could possibly look more foolish, Brandon made her get back to practice. She put on such a performance—shaking her butt, sticking out her breasts, flipping up her skirt—that Javier had to cover his face to hide his laughter.

Then Friday after the game, Sky's mom insisted that we go out and eat with them. I tried to make an excuse why we couldn't, but Javier jumped on the opportunity. He said Sky was more fun to laugh at than a gum-chewing jackass. At the restaurant, Mrs. Davis made a big production of reading the menu—rolling her *r*'s and putting way too much emphasis on some letters and not enough on others. Her Spanish is just terrible. I was afraid Javier would crack up laughing right then and there.

Sky thought she'd impress Javier by telling him everything she knew about Mexico, which took about a whole two minutes. Other than knowing that Acapulco is a great vacation spot and that the Aztecs made human sacrifices, she didn't know anything. So she started jabbering away about how her mom haggled with some peasant in Nuevo Laredo over the price of a blanket. She told Javier that he was "lucky to be one of the few elite in such a poor, pathetic country." That's when Javier's neck started to turn red around his collar. In my family, that's a sure sign that someone's getting angry. He excused himself to go to the restroom. Probably so that he could cool off. And, of course, Sky followed him, absolutely clueless that he was insulted. I'm beginning to think that girl has no shame. I thought Javier would let her have it with both barrels, but Sky came back glowing like she'd won an Oscar.

Grandmother and Javier left Sunday afternoon. Sky called no less than six times Saturday, to "see what I was doing." Finally, Mama told her that we were trying to visit with our family and to please stop calling.

Now we're back at school, and for two days, I've heard about nothing but Javier. Javier this, and Javier that. Sky tried to get his address from me so that she could write to him. I told her that where he lives, the mail is delivered by donkey only once a month, and that most of the time, it never gets there because the mailman is a drunk who takes siestas five times a day. Of course, I made all of that up. Sky believed me, though. It fit her image of Mexico and Mexicans, so why wouldn't she? She just sighed and mumbled something in Spanish under her breath. I must be mistaken, but I could have sworn she said "men's restroom."

Wednesday
October 16
Tiffany

Sage Mobley is trying to be my friend. She and John Keeler have been sitting with me at lunch every day this week. It's uncomfortable. I don't like to eat in front of people because of my overbite. I wonder what Sage wants from me. I wonder if she's part of some big joke and I won't know it until the punch line comes and everyone is standing around laughing in my face.

Sage seems okay. She isn't like most of the girls you meet in junior high. She hangs out with John all of the time, but she isn't a bit boy crazy. They're just friends. They don't act all goofy and do dumb stuff to try to impress each other. I don't really know all that much about Sage except that her mom is one odd duck.

I've seen her out front dropping Sage off for school. She wears nasty clothes and waves out of the window at the coaches. Maybe that's why Sage is being so nice. She knows what it's like to get embarrassed, and she feels sorry for me because I'm always tripping over my feet.

Even though I like Sage, she certainly doesn't need me for a friend. She's pretty, smart, and she has John, who is the best-looking boy in school. I don't want people trying to be my friend because they feel sorry for me. I'm not going to be someone's pathetic little "project."

So I keep things cordial by talking to them for a few minutes, and then I make an exit at the first opportunity. It really embarrasses me to have John sitting there. I just can't be around boys. Whenever I'm around one and I smile, I feel like the skin around my mouth is stretched as tight as a trampoline. My teeth are huge, and to make matters worse, I can actually feel every muscle in my face when I plaster on a fake smile.

Anyway, Spanish class was interesting today. Sky was all excited, waving her hand for Mr. Silva's attention. Then she said "Mr. Silva, what does *primada* mean? Does it mean 'first,' 'one and only,' what?" Mr. Silva asked her if she was sure that she was pronouncing it correctly. Sky said, "Of course I'm sure. It's written on my heart." Mr. Silva said, "Well, Sky, *primada* means 'stupid thing.' " Sky looked shocked. I can't figure out for the life of me why Sky Davis would have "stupid thing" written on her heart—it should be written on her forehead.

Thursday
October 17
Sage

I've been in a lousy mood all week. Last weekend, Dad and Carly had a barbeque to celebrate their marriage. Brandy and I were there, along with a bunch of Carly's relatives that we didn't even know and some of Dad's friends from work. Dad's friends were all clapping him on the back and congratulating him. Yes, sir, good old Jack Mobley traded in his used Plymouth for a brand-new Corvette. What a wheeler-dealer! *CONGRATULATIONS?!* How quickly those guys forgot the dinners Mom slaved over when they'd come over to watch football or the times Mom took them hot meals when their wives were away in the hospital having babies.

Carly's mom told us to call her Grandma Petty. I have two grandmas already, and I don't want another one, thank you very much. Of course I didn't tell her that. She was just trying to be nice. I felt sorry for her. It must have been kind of awkward for her too. After all, her daughter had an affair with a married man and broke up a family. That's not exactly what you'd want to brag about to your friends at the beauty parlor.

Dad had us all get together for a "family" picture. Maybe I'll get a copy for my old album. I'll call it "The Mobley family—Redefined." I hated every minute of the party. Carly called Brandy and me aside and told us, "Now that I'm your stepmom, you don't have to call me Carly anymore. You can call me something more familial, like Mom." Is she stupid or what? At that moment I could think of plenty of things to call Carly, but every one of them would have gotten me a week's restriction. Brandy looked so confused. She said, "But we already got a mom." I said, "That's right, Brandy. We do," and I grabbed her hand and walked her over for some punch and cookies.

Carly tried to apologize later. She said, "I just wasn't thinking. It slipped out. Too much champagne or something." I wonder if she "just wasn't thinking" when she got involved with someone else's husband. Why is it that people do things that are wrong and then try to pass it off as okay? Carly deliberately stole my dad right out from under my mom, and now we're supposed to love her like she's part of the family.

For a while after Dad moved out, I used to lie in bed and wonder what he and Carly had been thinking all those nights they were out sneaking around behind Mom's back. Didn't they even think about us at all? Didn't Dad feel ashamed knowing that we were at home believing that he was a great, hardworking dad putting in overtime at work? Didn't Carly imagine his wife and kids sitting down at the table without him, while she had his undivided attention over candlelight in some dark, out-of-the-way restaurant? I quit torturing myself with all of those questions. I finally decided that Dad and Carly just didn't care. That what *they* wanted was more important than anyone or anything else.

As if things weren't bad enough, Russell dumped Mom. Now she's out trying to find someone to "make *her* happy." Why don't we make her happy? Why didn't we make Dad happy? Brandy and I are good kids. We get good grades, brush our teeth, clean our rooms, and keep our elbows off the table. Do they have to have more? Couldn't all of their "happiness" have waited a few years until we were older? Couldn't they have given us a normal childhood?

MONDAY
OCTOBER 21
BRANDON

Laughinghouse is on my case 'cause I haven't been "journaling" enough. I think she's been doin' more than just "skimming through" this crap, cause she took me out in the hall the other day and talked to me about my vulgar language. Well, here goes some more interesting reading for Miss Laughinghouse's lonely weekend nights.

Pop is still all whacked out of shape over me being on the "queer squad." That's what he calls it. He and Mom had another one of their

"What-are-we-going-to-do-with-that-boy?" talks, and they've come up with the great idea that I should get a part-time job. I'll be 14 tomorrow; I was held back in first grade. Yep, failed the first grade. That's 'cause that was the year my real dad bailed on us, and I kinda just shut down for a while. So Pop has this buddy from the VFW that owns the movie theater. Without even askin' me, they have it all lined up for me to start work on Saturday.

I get to scrub the toilets and clean up everybody's candy wrappers after they leave the theater. That place is so gross, your shoes stick to the floor when you walk down the aisle. It won't be all bad. At least I won't have to hang around here on weekends and watch Pop swill beer in front of the television. I can make me some money, buy some tight new threads, and maybe even hit on the high school babes when they come in to see a flick.

If Miss Laughinghouse *ever* gets a date, maybe she and her stud can come catch a movie, and I'll get to watch them makin' out in the dark. Ha! Caught ya "skimming," didn't I?

Tuesday
October 22
Joanne

Sky and I had it out over Javier. When she found out that he had called her a "stupid thing," she demanded that I tell her what else he had said about her. I tried to be nice about it. I told her that he just wasn't interested because he already had a girlfriend back home. She wasn't buying. She kept on about "how dare he call her 'stupid' and a 'thing.' " Then she got personal. She said that her parents weren't crazy about her liking him anyway, because of the "ethnic thing." She said, "You know, he's a Mexican, and my family doesn't believe in dating people from other races. Besides, he probably doesn't come from the same class of people, being that he's from such a pathetic country."

That's when I quit being nice. I've taken Sky's subtle insults long enough. I told her that the real reason that Javier didn't like her was because the only thing she knows anything about is *Sky*. That no one likes to listen to another person brag about their money, their looks, and their stupid old Momma! I was so mad, that I just said anything that I could think of to hurt her. I told her she was bossy, shallow, and spoiled. Then I turned around and walked away.

I tried to apologize after I'd cooled off. She and the others were out in the courtyard at lunch, and I walked over to sit with them like I always do. Sky had already gotten to them. They all got up and started walking away when I sat down. That's when Sky turned toward me and held out a tube of Barbie Lip Gloss. She said, "I think you left this at my house, Joanne." All of the kids who were standing around started getting closer. You could hear the tension in Sky's voice. Everyone probably thought they were about to see a cat fight. Julia and Courtney just looked at the ground, like they were uncomfortable. Candice was right in there, backing Sky up.

I said, "That's not mine." Sky said, "Sure it is, Joanne. None of the rest of us buy our makeup at the Dollar Store." Then she dropped the lipstick on the ground and said, "Don't leave your trash laying around my house." She flipped her hair over her shoulder as she glided off. People were snickering. I was embarrassed. Not because I care one bit where people think I buy my makeup, but because I had stood there and let Sky treat me like dirt. This wasn't one of those little arguments that would pass over in a few days. Sky had drawn an invisible line between me and the others, showing me and everyone else that I didn't belong with them. After seeing how they all stood behind Sky, I realize that maybe I never did.

Wednesday
October 23
Tiffany

The school nurse called Mom on Monday. Miss Laughinghouse told her that I squint when I'm reading or writing. I was afraid that Mom was going to make me get glasses. But Mom let me get contacts! Colored ones. They're aqua, and they make my eyes an awesome color. We got them at the eyeglass place in the mall. And get this: While we were there, Mom gave me $50 to buy whatever I wanted. I bought makeup and got my ears pierced. I decided that I don't have to look as bad as I do. I mean, there isn't anything I can do about my teeth right now; the orthodontist wants to wait until all of my permanent molars are in. But I can fix up what little I do have.

Mom was excited. Last night after I'd gone to bed, I heard her tell Dad that she thinks I'm finally "coming out of my shell." I've been telling her about the things Sage, John, and I talk about at lunch. This time she actually believes that I'm talking to real people instead of lying to keep her happy. Then today, when I wanted makeup and earrings, she was beaming all over the place. I'll never be Marilyn. But, I can make Mom happy sometimes too.

I've decided that Sage isn't up to anything by being my friend. She, John, and I have lunch every day and talk about whatever. It's nice having friends. Sage's mom has been sad lately over a breakup with some guy, and Sage is a little strung out over it. I feel sorry for her. You can tell she loves her mom (even though she is really weird).

Sage and John want me to go to the Fall Festival on Halloween, but I don't think I will. I feel out of place in crowds. Besides, John likes Joanne, and he wants to ask her along as his date. That would be awkward. I still don't know how to act around her. What would Sky and all of her buddies say if she were hanging out with John, Sage, and me? I can't see that happening. What I can see is John and Sage joining their group for the night and leaving me standing in the corner by myself.

Anyway, I'm going to wear my new contacts to school tomorrow, *and* I'm going to put on a little mascara and some lip gloss. I also bought some new ponytail holders so I can pull my hair back and show off my earrings. I'm kind of nervous about fixing myself up, if you want to know the truth. It's like, if you don't try to look nice and people make fun of you, it isn't as bad as if you *do* try and they make fun of you. I don't really know how to explain it. I guess as long as people don't think you care about how you look, then they won't be as likely to make fun of you about it. I hope that people notice, and then I hope they don't.

Thursday
October 24
Sage

I could just strangle Sky Davis. She is the meanest, snobbiest, most vile person on the face of the earth! Tiffany got all fixed up for school today. She had on makeup, earrings, colored contacts, the whole works. If you ask me, she was really cute. Tiffany thinks she's so ugly, but she isn't. She has a little button nose and the deepest dimples I've ever seen.

We were sitting at our table at lunch, laughing about a story Mrs. Clark told us in social studies yesterday, when up walked Sky and her disciples. Sky leaned up close to Tiffany's face and said, "My, my, my, are those little turtle earrings? Oh, girls, isn't that just the cutest thing?" You could see Tiffany closing up inside of herself. Her smile vanished. She just stared at her mashed potatoes and waited for whatever came next. Sky's buddies giggled, and that gave her the encouragement she needed. She said, "And makeup too. I thought there was a law against testing cosmetics on lab rats."

Tiffany picked up her tray and walked away toward the door. Sky started to walk off too, but John stood up and caught her by the arm. When she turned around, she was smiling like an angel. I think that for a minute she thought John was going to ask her on a date or kiss her or something. Then she saw his face. He was so mad. I've never seen John like that before. He said, "Sky, you are an empty-headed, arrogant witch!" She yanked her arm away and screamed—I mean screamed—"How dare you touch me, John Keeler! I'll sue you for assault." That's when Principal Williams came running over and took both of them to the office. Sky didn't get into one bit of trouble. John was put in the in-school suspension room for two days. He can't eat with us or go to any of his regular classes. He has to be in there with all of the troublemakers from 8:00 to 4:00. Poor John.

I went to the courtyard to find Tiffany. She wasn't under the tree reading or hiding out behind the Coke machine. I found her in the bathroom scrubbing off her makeup and crying. I didn't know what to say, so I hugged her and walked out. I had to go someplace to be alone. I wanted to scream, kick, or hit something. Where do people like Sky get off?

What are her parents like? Didn't anyone ever tell her that it is wrong to make fun of people? And what about those girls who follow her around and laugh at her cruel jokes? Do they really think that's okay? Are they just like her, or are they just too stupid to think for themselves?

Last year, we learned about the Holocaust in reading class. We read *The Diary of Anne Frank*. Our teacher told us about how Hitler killed all of those people just because they were Jews. When we were learning about it, I kept trying to figure out how one man got so many other people to act on his own hate. I mean, you can believe that *one* person could be that crazy, but he had hundreds of people helping him. Maybe all of those people were like Sky's friends, only of course Sky's friends aren't all *that* bad. But maybe they didn't really believe in what they were doing; they just did it because they were too weak to say no. I know it isn't all that simple, but isn't that where it starts?

Monday
October 28
Joanne

It was Brandon's turn to have practice at his house last Thursday. The afternoon was a major disaster. We were supposed to meet there at 4:00 and stay until 6:00. I wasn't prepared for Brandon's family or his home. He lives in a trailer park on Avenue S. I got there at about the same time as Candice, Julia, and Courtney. Brandon was waiting for us outside on a hammock strung between two clothesline poles. There wasn't a bit of shade anywhere, and it's still hot here this time of year. We pulled plastic lawn chairs around the hammock and sat there looking at one another. The other girls seemed uncomfortable around me. I think they felt bad about sticking with Sky the other day when she tried to humiliate me in the courtyard. But they didn't know what to say, and neither did I, so we all just sat there hemming and hawing about the heat and watching a mangy dog dig through the neighbor's garbage.

Sky showed up at 4:30. She's always 30 minutes late. When she got out of the car, she leaned back in the window and told her mom, "I'll be okay, Momma. I promise I won't even go in the house." Then she turned around and tiptoed through the yard like she was walking through a minefield. She made a big show of hugging all the other girls and ignoring me.

We started practice, and I thought everything was going fairly well. Then Brandon's mother came outside and brought us a plate of snacks and some cold drinks. She was wearing a big flowery kimono and had her hair in pink curlers. Sky couldn't resist having a little fun. She said, "Why, hello, Mrs. McCormick. I'm Sky Davis. So pleased to meet you." She stuck out her hand like she expected Brandon's mother to bow down and kiss it, but she just nodded politely and kept pouring the drinks into Styrofoam cups. Sky couldn't take being snubbed, so she kept on, "Your house is just lovely. Has it always been parked here, or did you move it in from someplace else?" Mrs. McCormick looked at her and said, "It's always been here." "Well," Sky went on, "the scenery is absolutely breathtaking. Wouldn't you say, girls? I mean, those plastic flowers in the pots along the fence are just too cute. Does Mr. McCormick collect old cars? He has just ever-so-many here on the lawn." Mrs. McCormick excused herself and started toward the house.

When she was just about to the door, she turned around like she'd just remembered something and said, "Sky Davis, are you Robert Davis's daughter?" Sky said, "Well, yes, ma'am, I sure am. He's a very important lawyer with Davis, Jones, Harper, and Steele. You've heard of him?" Mrs. McCormick said, "Heard of him? I dated him in high school. Good old Robert Davis. Well, you kids have fun." Then she went inside the trailer and closed the door. Sky stood staring after her, her eyes narrowed to slits. For a minute, she looked pure evil.

Brandon called us over to a clear area in the yard so we could practice building a pyramid. He wanted Sky to build the middle by getting on his shoulders. She was just about up when Brandon stepped backward, causing her to lose her balance. She fell headfirst onto the lawn. Brandon helped her up, laughing as he did. She was red in the face and mad as a hornet. She started to berate Brandon for being a "clumsy oaf," but then she noticed something wet in her hair. It was so gross. Sky had dog poop smashed into her hair all along the right side of her face. She started gagging and ran over behind a beat-up, tireless V.W. bus. We could hear her vomiting. It was almost enough to make me puke too.

We didn't know what to do about Sky. She wanted to go home, but she refused to go into the house to use the phone, so Brandon's mom ended up bringing a cordless to the yard. She dialed her mom and started crying into the phone, demanding that she come to get her "right this minute." That's when Brandon's dad came home. He drove up in an old brown pickup with one yellow door and a Confederate flag sticker in the back window. When he got out of the truck, you could tell he'd been drinking. He sort of swaggered across the yard on his way to the back door. He didn't even notice us until he was halfway there. He stopped dead in his tracks, belched, rubbed his stomach, and said, "Damn, one of you smells like crap!"

Brandon looked embarrassed and nervous all of a sudden. I think he may be a little afraid of his dad. They didn't seem to be on great terms. Neither of them said a thing to each other before his dad walked into the house.

Practice was obviously over, so we took turns calling our parents to come pick us up. Thank God I thought to wipe off the phone before I used it. Sky had gotten dog poop all over the earpiece.

Tuesday
October 29
Sky

What is this world coming to? Thursday, John Keeler attacked me for being nice to Tiffany Andrews. All I was doing was paying the poor little reject a compliment, and *wham*, he goes off like a loaded cannon. He must still be hurt over our breakup. Why else would he behave that way?

Then after school, I had to go to Brandon's house for cheer practice. Oh my God! He practically lives in the dump—junk cars and half-starved dogs running around his house. There were kids in diapers playing in the mud across the street. It was so disgusting. His parents look like one of those couples that go on talk shows and tell everyone they're first cousins or something.

Momma was terrified to leave me there. On the way over, we saw a bunch of dirty old men in sleeveless undershirts playing checkers at a broken-down card table. Momma was just sure I'd be kidnapped and ravaged. The other girls looked just as horrified as I was. Except Joanne. She probably felt right at home. After all, the neighborhood looked just like the ones in Mexico.

What a horrid day! John hurt my feelings, Brandon's tacky old mother lied and told everyone that she used to date Daddy, and I got dog mess in my hair. I just know that Brandon did it on purpose. He's such a jerk! I'm going to get even with him, I swear.

Oh, well, as they say, "The poor will always be with us." So since I have to share the planet with scum, I'll just try to concentrate on the finer things in life. The Fall Festival is this Friday night. It's on Halloween, so it will be a masquerade. I already have my costume. I can't wait to show it off. I'm going with Stephen. He's the quarterback of our football team. I added him to our approved list just yesterday. That's when he asked me to the dance. Stephen isn't very bright. He's also from a family that doesn't quite fit our ticket.

But he is the quarterback, and he just adores me. I'm going to make John Keeler so jealous. He thought he'd get to me over the Joanne thing, but it didn't work. I haven't seen them say one word to each other. Maybe there's a language barrier. I don't think John speaks Mexican.

Thursday
October 31
Tiffany

Sage and John have talked me into going to the Fall Festival tomorrow night. I can't believe I'm doing this. After what happened the other day, I told myself that I would, never, ever, ever, talk to anyone again. It's so much easier to hide than to risk trying to fit in. I'm not sure that I'm doing the right thing. But I made the mistake of telling Mom about the dance, and she wants me to go so badly that I just can't stand to disappoint her. To make matters worse, John's taking Joanne as his date. These past few weeks have been the happiest I've had in so long. What will I do if my new friends abandon me to hang out with Joanne's crowd?

And what if kids make fun of me? I've been made fun of a lot in my life, but it's even worse when people tease you in front of friends. When Sky started in on me at the table last Wednesday, I wanted to crawl in a hole and die. Part of me was sick with fear that Sage and John would join in with the others and laugh. They didn't, though. When Sage found me crying in the bathroom, she looked like she wanted to kill someone, and then John told Sky just exactly what she's always needed to hear. I hate it that John got in trouble. I told him I was sorry. He smiled and ruffled my hair. He didn't say anything at all. He didn't have to.

Anyway, I'm going to that stupid dance, but I'm going in disguise. Marilyn went to Debbie's School of Dance for years, and Mom kept all of her costumes. She actually unlocked the shrine and dug them out of Marilyn's closet so I could go through them. They're terrific! I picked a belly dancer costume, complete with a veil. That way, only my eyes will show, and the rest of my face will be hidden. Sage and I walked to the grocery store and bought some temporary hair color. No one will even know it's Tiffany the buck-toothed, dirty dishwater kid hiding under that veil. I'll be Sage's redheaded cousin Camille, visiting from out of state.

Sage is dressing like a lumberjack. She's going to wear hiking boots, a fur-lined cap, a flannel, and overalls. She bought a plastic ax from the Halloween aisle while we were shopping for my hair color. I offered to lend her one of Marilyn's dance costumes, but she turned it down. Sage isn't one to wear frilly stuff. We're going to get ready at Sage's house, and then John's dad is picking us up on his way back from Joanne's. That's the scary part. Joanne might recognize me. I think I can get away with being incognito at the dance because it'll be dark, but the ride over in the car is a little too close for comfort.

4
chapter

November

Classroom Jester. Teacher's bane.

Is he jolly? He's in pain.

Outer folly. Inner shame.

Do they hurt him?

Yes they do.

Will he take it?

Silly, you.

Joshua

Monday
November 4
Sage

It would have been a terrific Halloween if Brandy hadn't been hit by a car. When I got back from the dance, no one was home. I thought that was kind of weird because it was past 11:00, and trick-or-treating usually only lasts a little past dark. Mom's car was in the garage because she and Brandy were just going to walk around the neighborhood to collect candy.

I was sitting on the couch, worried sick, when a car pulled up out front. I looked out the window, and Mom was getting out of the passenger seat. My first thought was that she'd found a baby-sitter and gone on a date. I was about to really lose my temper when she opened the back door and scooped up poor little Brandy. I met them halfway down the sidewalk. Brandy was doped up from a shot they'd given her in the emergency room. She had a cast on her left arm and cuts and bruises all over her face. Her bumblebee costume was torn, and stuffing was poking out everywhere. Her face was streaked with tears, pink rouge, and eyeliner.

When we got into the house, Mom laid Brandy on the couch, collapsed into her recliner, and burst into tears. She was sobbing so hard, I could barely understand her. She said that she and Brandy had been trick-or-treating about four blocks over. They went to someone's door, and Mom got into a conversation. The next thing she knew, she heard brakes squealing and a terrible thud. There was Brandy lying in the street. The car that hit her hadn't been going all that fast because of all the trick-or-treaters running around. Thank God, or Brandy would be dead right now.

I don't know what came over me. I've never been disrespectful to my mother, but I just went ballistic. I screamed at her, "Who were you talking to, Mom? A man? Were you trying to score a date while your baby was running around in the street?" I told her other things too. I told her that she wasn't like a "real" mom. That she was an embarrassment to her children. That she needed to quit trying to make herself happy and take care of her kids. I could see that every word I said cut Mom to the bone, but I just couldn't stop myself. Then Brandy started to whimper, and

I burst into tears. We were all crying: Mom, because she had failed us; me, because at that moment, I hated my own mother more than anyone in the world; and Brandy, because she was hurt and afraid.

The rest of the weekend, I spoiled Brandy rotten. I couldn't get over thinking that had that car been going a little faster, I would have lost my little sister forever. I fluffed her pillows, made malts, played cards, and watched *Old Yeller* with her five times. Mom just shuffled around the house in her robe and slippers. She looks like she's lost her mind. I don't care. I want her to feel miserable. I know that Mom didn't cause the divorce. But neither did we. We've been hurting too, but she's been too busy licking her own wounds to even notice. It's time for her to wake up and remember that she has two kids that need her. I'm sick of being the only grown-up in this house. Every time Mom looks at Brandy, I want that swollen little face and broken arm to send a dagger through her heart.

Tuesday
November 5
Joanne

So much can change *en menos que canta un gallo*—"in less time than the rooster crows." One minute, Sage's little sister is laughing and buzzing around like a little bumblebee, and the next minute, she's all banged up. One day I'm friends with the most popular girls at Prescott, and the next, I'm friendless. And a few days later, I have a whole new set of friends, and I couldn't be happier. Life is truly unpredictable.

I went to the Fall Festival with John Keeler. He and his dad picked me up from my house at 7:00 on the dot. I'm glad they weren't late. I was so excited, I don't think I could have stood waiting another minute. I was ready by 6:30. I went dressed as a Mexican dancer. My mother used to dance with the Ballet Folklorico, so I dug one of her old dresses out of a trunk in the attic. The dress was bright orange with a slip that made the skirt poof way out. I found everything I needed in that trunk. There were tortoise-shell combs, lace scarves, rice-paper fans, castanets, and big buckled shoes. It was a great costume.

I told John what I was going to wear, so he went as a matador. He made his costume out of a tiny old tuxedo he'd worn in his aunt's wedding when he was eight. It worked out great. He had his mother sew gold buttons to the cuffs of his trousers, and he borrowed a frilly white shirt and white stockings. He cut a cape from a red wool blanket. When we were leaving my house, he laid it on the sidewalk for me to walk over like he was rolling out a red carpet. He is so funny.

After he picked me up, we went to Sage's house to get her and her "cousin" Camille. At first, I had no idea that Camille was really Tiffany. She had on a fantastic belly dancer costume. It had pink silk pantaloons and a little velvet vest just like the one Barbara Eden wears in *I Dream of Jeannie* on Nick at Nite. The veil covered most of her face. She had her hair piled up in a high ponytail of strawberry blonde ringlets. She was gorgeous. I would never have guessed that it was Tiffany just by looking. She had aqua eyes, and her brows were penciled in to perfection. "Camille" wasn't saying a word, so her voice didn't give her away. What tipped me off was that on the ride to the dance, every time someone said something funny, "Camille" would put her hand to her veil and laugh. That reminded me of someone. It took me about five minutes of beating my brains to think of who. And then it hit me. Tiffany has a habit of covering her mouth when she laughs or smiles because she's embarrassed of her overbite. Once I noticed that, I took a second look. It was definitely Tiffany. How could I not have known? The way her eyes squint into a smile when she's happy should have been a dead giveaway. I guess it had just been a really long time since I'd seen Tiffany happy. I didn't let them know that I knew. I went along with the game. Inside, I was bursting. Things couldn't have been better.

We had a blast at the dance. John and I danced slow songs alone, but when a fast song played, we all danced together. The DJ had some mariachi music, and I taught my new friends to dance the way Papa had taught me. Tiffany was a hit. No one but us ever knew it was her. When she wasn't dancing with us, she had guys lining up to ask her. It was like a Cinderella story: "Tiffany Rises from the Ashes and Becomes the Belle of the Ball."

Sky was there. She was with Stephen Johnson, our quarterback. Stephen is kind of slow—mentally. He can also be mean sometimes. He's the one that picks on Brandon the most, calling him bad names. He's not bad-looking, though, and he's a sharp dresser, so he fits Sky's ticket close enough. Even so, she ignored him most of the night except when she had him running back and forth to the snack table to get her a refill of punch. He followed her around like a puppy all night while she flitted from person to person, making witty comments.

She came prancing up to us, dressed like a princess, of course, and said, "Oh, Joanne, your costume, how ethnically charming." Then she glared at John for a few seconds. No doubt she wanted him to say something so she could sic Fido on him. But John just stood there smiling like the joke was on her, so she stomped off dragging Stephen by his invisible leash.

Brandon showed up late. He was wearing an old football uniform—probably his Dad's. It was way too big. He had torn off the old numbers and glued a big construction-paper 16 on in their place. Stephen is number 16.

Brandon rolled the bottom of his jersey up past his navel, tiptoed around like Tinkerbelle, and drank his punch with his pinkie finger extended. He even went so far as to get on the dance floor behind Stephen and start dancing. Stephen spun around and tried to hit him, but Brandon was too fast. He ducked and ran away on tippy toes, giggling like a girl.

I was sad when the night was over. John's dad picked us up. They dropped me off first. When we were about a block from my house, I said, "I wish Tiffany Andrews had been at the dance. I miss her. She was the best friend I ever had." "Camille" just stared out of her window. John and Sage looked at me with a knowing smile.

I had the best time ever. I went to bed that night feeling warm and happy. I dreamed I was a beautiful señorita watching my matador battle an ugly black bull. The bull was wearing a diamond-studded tiara.

Wednesday
November 6
Sky

I would like to say that I had fun at the Fall Festival. But thanks to SOME people, I had a horrible time. It's such a shame too, because I had the best costume at the dance. I wore a gold taffeta gown with a sheer jewel-studded overlay. Momma and I bought it a store that specializes in costumes. The salesman said that I was the perfect girl for the gown. That lots of other girls had tried it on, but I was the only one who had done it justice. It cost a fortune, but how could we pass it up? It was made for me. Daddy pitched a fit, of course. He said that we could have dug up something around the house for a Halloween costume and saved $200. He is just being ridiculous. I will not "dig something up" to wear to a dance. I'm beginning to think that Daddy is losing his mind.

We also bought a pair of gold slippers and a scepter. But the best part of my costume was my tiara. It looked just like the one Miss America wore last year at the pageant. It had three rows of faux diamonds. Whenever I moved, the light would glance off the cut glass and throw sparkles everywhere. Stephen said that I was just the most beautiful girl he'd ever seen. He called me "Princess" all evening. Which, I must say, began to wear on my nerves just a bit.

Stephen is okay, I guess. It's just that all night, he didn't give me any room to mingle. Every time I turned around, there he was. I had to send him away to get me punch if I wanted to get any space at all. His dad is rather rude too. They came to pick me up at 7:00, and I wasn't ready. Momma says that you should always keep boys waiting. You don't want to look like an eager beaver. His dad acted like it was really putting him out to have to wait 30 minutes. Momma said he kept sighing and looking at his watch, which hurt her feelings because she was trying to show him her antique pewter collection. You'd think he would appreciate the opportunity to see something so valuable. After all, Stephen's family isn't exactly what I'd consider wealthy.

As I was saying, I would have had a good time if it hadn't been for Joanne, John, Brandon, and some little snot that Sage Mobley brought along. First of all, I can't believe that Joanne would go to the dance with John. Sure, we've had a few disagreements lately, but she is supposed to be my friend, and she knows that I like him. You would think that after all we've been through together, she wouldn't want to hurt me like that. They looked ridiculous together, by the way. The very idea of dressing so Mexican for the dance. It was like she was flaunting it or something. I think that her uppity cousin Javier must have put ideas in her head while he was here visiting. Some people just can't accept their place in life. Sure, he and his family may be somebodies in Mexico, but how hard is that? If you're the only person with a dollar to your name in an entire country, then I guess you *would* think rather highly of yourself.

Then there was that girl that came with Sage—her cousin or something. She thought she was the cat's meow. You should have seen her prancing around with a gang of boys in tow. I guess she didn't realize that the only reason they were interested was because she wasn't from here. The "new girl in town" always gets attention at first, even if she's as ugly as homemade soap. This girl had half her face covered for goodness' sake. No telling what she was hiding under there. She could have been the bearded lady from the carnival for all those boys knew. But there she was, getting all of the attention, even though everyone could *see* my face and they *know* how beautiful I am. I just can't figure these people out. I asked Momma about it, and she said that it was probably because the little tramp's costume showed her belly. Momma says that boys will chase after a pig if it's showing enough skin. I don't know why Principal Williams even allowed her to stay at the dance dressed in that skimpy outfit!

And Brandon! He has gone too far this time. He dressed up in a football uniform with Stephen's number and then acted like a drag queen all night. Why he wants to irritate Stephen, I'll never know. Brandon is a fool. Stephen could kill him with one punch. And you wouldn't think that Brandon would play around like he's gay with all the rumors flying around about him. Maybe he really is gay, and he wants to come out of the closet. Who knows? Maybe he has a crush on Stephen. Oh, God! Wouldn't that be awful? Maybe that's why he got on the cheer squad in the first place—so he could be closer to the guys. What is this world coming to? Minorities and homosexuals running around advertising their diversity, outsiders coming to OUR dance and trying to steal the show, boys being on the cheer squad. Everything has just turned inside out. What happened to the good old days, when beautiful, normal girls were appreciated?

Thursday
November 7
Tiffany

I am a mystery. No one knows that I was the veiled dancer at the Fall Festival. No one except Sage and John, of course. And maybe Joanne. But everyone else is still talking and wondering about Sage's cousin. Several boys have asked her when "Camille" was coming back to visit. Oh, what fun it was being Camille. If only I could be that brave all of the time. I danced and flirted, just like other girls, and I really enjoyed it. I mean, really!

The dance was great, but it seems we're all paying a price in one way or another for our night of fun. Sage feels guilty because Brandy got hurt. She says that if she'd been there, Brandy wouldn't have been running around in the street. I'm a little sad because now that I've tasted what it was like to be Camille, I like being Dishwater Drucilla even less. And Joanne is really catching it for going to the dance with John.

Yesterday in Spanish, Mr. Silva asked Joanne to run up to the office to make him some copies of a quiz. He gave her a hall pass which happens to be a green slip of paper. No sooner did Joanne have the pass in her hand then Sky called out, "Look, everybody, Joanne finally got her green card." Joanne slammed the door on her way out. Several people laughed. Mr. Silva didn't think it was very funny. He went into a lecture about bigotry. He told us that he had immigrated to the United States from Mexico when he was ten, and their lives had been tough. They were discriminated against: called wetbacks, paid less than the minimum wage, forced to pay higher rent than others, etc. He glared at Sky while he told his story. If she wants to pass Spanish, I don't think she'll be making any more "green card" jokes in Mr. Silva's class.

Anyway, Saturday afternoon, Sage and I are going to take Brandy to a new movie that's showing at the cinema. It's rated G, and it's animated, but it'll be fun to get out of the house even if the movie is for little kids.

Sunday
November 10
Sage

A couple of hours ago, this man came knocking on the door. He was an older guy, probably about 40, and nice-looking in a dignified kind of way. He was wearing a suit and tie. At first I was afraid he might be a salesman, so I wasn't sure if I should open the door, but he had a great big teddy bear in one arm and a box of candy in his hand. He looked nervous. Turned out, he was the man who had hit Brandy on Halloween. He said that he had been meaning to come by all week, but he wasn't sure if he should. Then after a meeting at church, he got up the nerve to stop by. He'd been carrying the bear and the candy around in his car for days.

He felt so terrible about the whole thing. He told me that he didn't see Brandy until it was too late—that she'd just come out of nowhere, and he didn't have time to stop. He said that this was the worst thing that had ever happened to him in his life. That when he hit her, his heart stopped. He thought that he'd killed her. I asked him to come in the house and sit down, and then I brought Brandy in to see him. She went right over to him and hugged him. I didn't know until that moment that he was also the person who had rushed Brandy and Mom to the hospital that night. He told me the whole story. How Mom had been like a zombie on the way to the hospital, how she kept saying over and over, "My baby, my baby." He had to take over in the emergency room. Mom wasn't able to give the doctors much information, and she was so hysterical that they didn't want her to go back to the examining room with Brandy. He'd gone instead.

He gave Brandy the bear and the candy and signed her cast. He asked how Mom was doing, and I told him she was okay. I didn't want to tell him that she had barely gotten out of bed all week. That, in fact, she was in bed at that very moment. He was already feeling like this was all his fault, even though there was no way he could have avoided the accident. He really was a nice man.

Other than the visit from Mr. Evans, (That's his name. I had to get it from Brandy's cast after he left because I'd forgotten to ask.) nothing's changed. Mom's still in bed. I don't know if she'll ever snap out of this. I'm starting to feel a little sorry for her. Dad married Carly, Russell dumped her, and Brandy got hit by a car, all in one month. I guess all of that could push anyone over the edge.

Tiffany and I took Brandy to the movies on Saturday. Sky and Stephen were there, making noise and being rude. Why they were at a rated G movie, I don't know. Probably because Stephen has a six-year-old mentality. Brandon McCormick works at the theater. I didn't know that until I saw him walking around the lobby with a broom and a dustpan. He looked serious for a change. A man with a job to do. Who would have thought that Brandon worked? Evidently, Sky hadn't known he worked there either. I heard she and Stephen having a good laugh over it while we were waiting in line to buy popcorn. They were way up in front of us, but Sky made sure that everyone could hear what they were talking about. She was telling Stephen that Brandon lived in a junkyard and that his mother buys groceries with food stamps. Sky is so hateful! When they turned to go back into the theater, they spotted us. Sky started laughing so hard, she had to lean on Stephen to keep from falling over. Stephen must have thought she was terribly cute guffawing like a jackass and spewing popcorn all over the place. He laughed too, though he looked like he didn't have a clue what was so funny. He's as dumb as a brick.

Tiffany whispered that she hated Sky, and Brandy overheard. She's heard John and me talk about Sky before, but she'd never seen her. Poor Brandy didn't know any better. She's always listening in on our conversations, and sometimes she hears things that she shouldn't. She said, "Sage, is that the hateful bish?" Sky stopped laughing and stared at Brandy. She was about to blow. She looked scary. Her face went beet red, and she had a popcorn kernel stuck in the corner of her mouth. She said, "What did you say, you little brat?" Brandy ducked behind me and clung to my leg with her good arm. I stood there ready for anything. I guess Sky could tell by the look on my face that she'd better back down. So she did. She and Stephen got about five steps from us, and Sky turned around to make her parting shot. She said, "Pageboy Sage and Buck-Tooth Tiffany. What a couple of rejects."

MONDAY
NOVEMBER 11
BRANDON

Me and Pop had a fight. I came home from work on Saturday really ticked. He met me at the door raisin' hell 'cause I hadn't taken the trash out before I left. I asked him why *he* couldn't take out the trash, seeing as how he doesn't do crap all day but sit on his butt or hang out with his buddies and play cards. He slapped me. That's the first time he's ever hit me. He looked sorry as soon as he'd done it. Too late, though. Mom hasn't said a word to him since it happened. I got a busted lip, and one of my teeth is loose.

The reason I was in such a mood on Saturday in the first place, was 'cause of that two-bit wench Sky Davis and her moron boyfriend. They came to the theater and started makin' jokes about me workin' there. She was even talkin' crap about my mother. That's where I draw the line. My mom's the nicest lady in this lousy town. It's not her fault my real dad dumped her and now she's gettin' raked over by Pop. She has to clean people's houses and baby-sit all day to scrape together a few bucks. She goes to the grocery store late at night so no one will know she has to use welfare to get our food. Then Sky, who's so spoiled she's never even had to wipe her own butt, yells it out in the lobby for everyone and his dog to hear.

That's not all Sky did. She and the moron left crap all over the place at the movie 'cause they knew I'd have to clean it up. They poured cola and popcorn all over the floor and stuck a Slo Poke to the seat. It took me a good 20 minutes just to clean their mess. One of these days, Sky's gonna get what she has coming, and I may just be the one to give it to her.

Tuesday
November 12
Joanne

Tiffany and I are friends again. At least, I think we are. She didn't say anything, like, "Hey, Joanne, do you want to be friends again?" But that wouldn't be Tiffany's way. She smiled at me, though, in Spanish class. I finally blew my cover and started rattling off whole paragraphs to Mr. Silva. He didn't look a bit surprised, like I thought he would. I think he knew all along that I was faking.

On our way out of class, Sky whispered, "Wet" under her breath and gave me her best go-to-you-know-where look. Then Tiffany looked me right in the face and smiled. It was great. My life is finally becoming my own again.

Wednesday
November 13
Tiffany

The funniest thing happened today. Sky Davis walked down the hall with a Slo Poke stuck to her butt. I have no idea where it came from. We don't have candy machines at school anymore. Not since last year. Mr. Williams had them taken out because kids were leaving wrappers all over the place. But there she was, wearing a plaid miniskirt with a big, sticky caramel Slo Poke stuck on her left butt cheek. The part of the wrapper that said Slo Poke was still hanging off the candy, which made it even funnier because it kind of made a statement. Sky's never in a hurry. Everywhere she goes, she ambles along like she's modeling the outfit of the day. So there she was, sashaying down the hall, doing her runway walk, and all the kids behind her were cracking up.

Someone must have tipped her off to what was so funny, because she let Brandon McCormick have it after fifth period. She thought he had something to do with it. He probably did. Anyway, she caught him over by his locker and told him that he'd embarrassed her for the last time. She said he was "gonna get it." Then she went crying to Stephen and made the biggest scene you ever saw. Sky can really act. She threw herself into Stephen's arms, buried her face in his shirt, and wailed. All of that carrying on over a Slo Poke on her butt seemed pretty dramatic to me, but Stephen was hugging her, wiping away her tears, and shooting looks at Brandon like he wanted to rip his guts out.

Monday
November 18
Joanne

Something terrible has happened. Thursday after school we all got together at Courtney's for cheerleading practice. Brandon didn't show. When we were leaving school, he told Julia that he'd be there a few minutes late because he had to walk to the theater to pick up his paycheck. Sky was 30 minutes late, as always, so it was just four of us for a while. We didn't really start to wonder about Brandon until 5:00 rolled around and he still hadn't shown up. It was the first time he'd missed a practice. Sky said that it just went to show how "some people don't take their obligations seriously."

Sky didn't seem one bit concerned about Brandon. The rest of us were a little worried. He had come to school with a busted lip on Monday, and we'd all secretly been wondering if things were worse at home than Brandon let on. He jokes around sometimes about how much his stepdad hates him, but he doesn't act like it's really a big deal. Julia, Courtney, Candice, and I were all thinking maybe his stepdad had done something to him and that's why he hadn't shown up.

Sky couldn't have been happier. She took over Brandon's position and led practice. She said that she should have been head cheerleader in the first place, so it was only right. We all had a chance to see what things would have been like had Brandon not won the lead position. I don't think we ever appreciated him as much as we did that day. Sky called all of the shots. She wouldn't take any suggestions from the rest of us, and she found something to criticize about everything we did. Especially me, since I'm no longer one of "the gang." By the time 6:00 rolled around, even Candice was sick of Sky. That's unusual because she's always been the one to worship Sky the most. Practice wasn't one bit of fun without Brandon.

I didn't find out what had happened until later that night when Sage called. She said that Mrs. Clark had been walking home when she found Brandon out in the field behind school. He was unconscious and badly beaten. He had to be taken to the hospital in an ambulance, and, according to Sage—who heard it from John, who heard it from his mom who's a nurse at the hospital—Brandon almost died. He had a ruptured spleen, a lacerated bladder, a broken nose, and both of his hands were smashed. No one knows exactly what happened. The doctor said that it looked as if someone had punched and kicked him repeatedly. Sage and I talked for over an hour, trying to figure out who could have done it. Sure, Brandon can be annoying, and his practical jokes sometimes go a little far, but he's not a mean person, and he certainly didn't deserve to be maimed.

The next day at school, everyone was talking about what happened. Some people thought Brandon's stepdad had beaten him, but that didn't make sense. Why would his stepdad come to school to beat him up? Principal Williams called some kids into his office to ask questions. We were all called in: me, Candice, Sky, Courtney, and Julia. He asked us if we knew anything, and of course, we didn't. Sky started crying in his office. She said, "The whole thing is just so horrible. Why would anyone do such a thing?" I thought it was kind of weird the way she went on. You would have thought she and Brandon had been best friends instead of archenemies. I thought that maybe she felt guilty for the way she'd treated him. But then after we talked to Mr. Williams, Courtney suggested that we not cheer at the game that night. As sort of a tribute to Brandon. Sky suddenly forgot about how broken up she was. She said that was the dumbest idea she'd ever heard. She said, "We don't need Brandon. There are five of us. We can cheer without him." She was missing the whole point. Julia tried to make her understand that it wouldn't seem right to go on and cheer with Brandon all laid up in the hospital fighting for his life. Sky finally lost her temper and yelled, "I'm cheering at that game tonight, with or without the rest of you!"

I went to the game with John. We sat with Tiffany, Sage, and Brandy. Our team played worse than they had all season. Two of our players, including Stephen, didn't even play. They were sick and hadn't come to school that day. Sky did exactly what she'd said she would do. She cheered on the sidelines all by herself. I don't think she had a clue how silly she looked. She was having the time of her life. Sky hates to share the limelight with anyone, and this time, she didn't have to. She was a one-woman show.

Tuesday
November 19
Sky

I don't know why everyone is so up in arms over Brandon McCormick. So what? He got his butt kicked. It isn't like he didn't have it coming. After all, if there is anyone at Prescott that deserved it, it's that idiot! For God's sake, it's not like he's going to die! I think he's faking like he's hurt worse than he is. He'll probably just lie around in the hospital for a few days and get every iota of attention that he possibly can. Then he'll come right back to school and start tormenting me again.

I can't believe how my own friends are acting over this. I suppose they thought they were being noble by refusing to cheer at the homecoming game. If you ask me, our football players deserve our support a whole lot more than that low-life Brandon. It was all up to me to support the team. I didn't need them anyway; I put on a fine performance all by myself. The thing that got me was that all the other cheerleaders were at the game watching. I saw Joanne sitting in the stands with John. She probably didn't really give a fig about Brandon. All that "Let's not cheer as a tribute to our fallen buddy" crap was just an excuse so she could be with her boyfriend instead of on the field living up to her obligations. Some people will use anything as an excuse to avoid responsibility.

And another thing, people have been looking at me funny. They don't think I notice, but I see them glancing at me out of the corner of their eyes. I know what they're all thinking. Just because I hate Brandon's guts doesn't mean that I had anything to do with what happened to him. I'm sure lots of people hate Brandon just as much as I do. Maybe it was the teachers that jumped him. Maybe it was The Tank. She's big enough to whip a grown man, and she can't stand Brandon either. Or maybe it was his stepdad. Lord knows that man is creepy enough. He's probably a serial killer out on parole from the penitentiary. Who knows? Why did Principal Williams call the cheer squad into his office anyway? What could we possibly know about it? The rest of us cheerleaders were practicing like we were supposed to be. All I know is that no one had better try to say I had anything to do with this. My daddy is an attorney. I'll sue for defamation of character!

Wednesday
November 20
Sage

This past weekend, Brandy and I went camping with Dad and Carly. The weather has gotten cold, and Brandy still has her cast, so we couldn't swim, but we did a lot of hiking. When we got home on Sunday, the house was spotless, and Mom had rearranged all the furniture. I thought, "Oh, boy, here we go. Mom's met another man." But she hadn't. She hadn't even left the house all weekend, except to go to the grocery store for cleaning supplies. I was surprised. When we'd left on Friday, Mom was still slinking around in her bathrobe.

Then I figured out what had brought on the sudden change. I usually leave this journal in the top left drawer of my dresser, underneath my T-shirts. It wasn't there. I found it in the top right drawer under my jeans. At first, I was upset. I've written a lot of things in this journal about Mom. I went back and reread everything, just to be sure I didn't say anything too absolutely terrible. But all that I wrote was how I feel about the divorce and the way she's changed. I didn't want to hurt her feelings, but I'm glad she knows. She hasn't mentioned that she read my journal, and neither have I. I suppose that all I needed to say has been said. Mom doesn't need to say anything either. She fried chicken and made mashed potatoes for Sunday dinner, and then she played Monopoly with us until bedtime. That says enough.

Brandon McCormick is still in the hospital. People at school are so worked up over it that no one is talking about anything else. The whole town is in an uproar. This place is small, so when something like this happens, it's a big deal. Until last week, kids walked everywhere here. We walked to our friends' houses, Pizza Hut, Wal-Mart, the theater, just about anyplace we wanted to go. But now, kids who only live a few blocks from the school are being car-pooled. Parents are afraid. If Brandon would just tell who beat him up, everyone could breathe easier, but he's not saying. He says he can't remember. John's mom is a nurse at the hospital. She said that Brandon didn't suffer any brain damage, so the doctors can't understand his memory loss.

They just don't know Brandon. Over the years, I've seen how he is about telling on people. Because Brandon's a clown, teachers naturally blame him when someone plays a prank. Several times, lucky pranksters have gotten off scot-free while Brandon did detention or in-school suspension for their crimes. Like last year, Greg Cuellar put a whoopee cushion in Mr. Holladay's desk chair. Holladay is one of those guys who definitely can't take a joke. He was so mad that he stuttered when he called Brandon into the hall. "B—B—Brandon, g—g—g—get your butt out here!" We all thought when Holladay lowered the boom on Brandon, he'd tell Holladay that it was Greg who'd done it. We'd all seen Greg stick it in Holladay's chair while he was in the hall hanging out the attendance folder. So Greg was holding his breath, waiting for the ax to fall, when Mr. Holladay came back into the room alone. Rather than tell who really did it, Brandon had taken the rap. He and Greg weren't even friends. I just thought Brandon liked jokes so much that he didn't mind claiming them, even when they weren't his. But what happened to him last week was no joke, and Brandon still refuses to "snitch." I don't know if he's stubborn or just stupid.

THURSDAY
NOVEMBER 21
BRANDON

I've got a busted nose, my guts are all bashed in, and I have three broken fingers. So, Miss Laughinghouse, you're probably wondering how in the heck I'm writing this journal. Well, I suppose you and all my other heartless teachers could have asked yourselves that BEFORE you sent a mountain of homework to the hospital with Liver Lips Williams. A guy can't even get a break when he's on his freakin' deathbed.

If it weren't for my hot secretary, none of you would be getting a thing from me. Would you make me repeat the seventh grade just because I got rolled? How fair is that? Crap, at the rate you teachers would have me getting through school, I'd be collecting social security before I got my diploma. Here I am, laid out like a corpse, and you people expect me to: memorize the U.S. Constitution, complete exercises A–Z in my language arts book, translate the American Standard Dictionary, and solve world hunger.

Other than being assigned a ton of homework by sadistic taskmasters, being in the hospital isn't such a bad deal. I have one really hot nurse who brings me my breakfast. This morning I told her that I had a pain way down in my throat. I opened wide, and she leaned in for a look. The view was incredible.

I refuse to take any more dictation until Brandon quits being a pig—*Courtney*

Thursday
November 21
Joanne

We were supposed to have cheer practice yesterday, but instead Julia, Candice, Courtney and I went to the hospital to see Brandon. It was the first time I'd seen him since he'd gotten hurt. Courtney goes just about every day. I was shocked. He has bruises all around his eyes, his nose is swollen, and he has bandages on his hands. His insides are so messed up, he can't even get out of bed to go to the bathroom. They have something called a catheter attached to him, you know—down there. He wanted to show it to us, but we threatened to leave if he took off his blanket. Even all beaten up like that, Brandon is still a clown.

He asked about Sky. Why she didn't come with us. He was being sarcastic, of course. Brandon knows that Sky hates him. Julia asked him why he wouldn't tell who beat him up. Brandon said he can't remember. We all knew he was lying. I told him that if he told, the police would make sure they didn't hurt him anymore. He was really offended. He said, "Is that why you think I won't tell? 'Cause I'm scared? Listen, sister, it ain't about that. I'm not tellin' cause I ain't a snitch." I'm sorry, but that is the dumbest thing I ever heard, and I told him so. Sometimes, Brandon is just too odd to figure out. One day he's acting like a girl to make everyone laugh, then the next he's trying to be Jackie Chan—Mr. Tough Guy. I think maybe some of his stepdad has rubbed off on him.

Speaking of Brandon's stepdad, he showed up when we were just about to leave. He seemed a lot different than when we'd seen him at Brandon's house. He stood just inside the door of the hospital room with his baseball cap in his hands. He looked like he wasn't sure whether to come in or run for it. He mumbled something about going to Auto Zone and the hospital being on his way home. He asked, "You need anything, son?" Brandon said, "Yeah, you can bring me a Big Mac, some fries, a malt, and a *Playboy*." His stepdad just laughed, and so did Brandon. Then his stepdad left, and Brandon got this weird look on his face. Weird for Brandon, because he rarely looks serious. We said our good-byes and left him to his thoughts.

Monday
November 25
Tiffany

I found this freaky note in my locker this morning. Not a note, really, a poem, written on a piece of blue notebook paper. It goes like this:

Evening.
Sun's faded.
Lone Jester.
Unaided.
Terror. Fright.
Menacing number in the night.

November

Rotten Queen
Cheers it on.
Lethal blows he casts upon
The lone jester.

Alone.
Unworried.
Previously unhurried.
Princess calls the shots
How much pain shall we allot?
Apple Pie! Banana Split!
The jester's going to get a hit!
Shake him to the left!
Shake him to the right!
He won't be practicing tonight.

Wait.

Unmoving.
What is the violence proving?
Twenty minus four
Starts to wonder what it's for
And
stops.
Horror, fright
Fearful number in the night.
Gone too far
No turning back.
Rotten Queen
Your heart is black.

I've thought about it all day. Who left it? What's it supposed to mean? And why did the poet leave it in my locker?

Tuesday
November 26
Sage

Yesterday after school, Tiffany came over. She had a poem that someone had slipped through the vents in her locker. The first couple of times we read it, it didn't make any sense. All of that stuff about a "lone jester" and a "queen"? Then Tiffany recognized some of the lines: "Apple Pie! Banana Split!" That was part of the cheer Sky did at tryouts. Then the next lines: "The jester's going to get a hit! Shake him to the left! Shake him to the right! He won't be practicing tonight." Of course, the jester is Brandon McCormick. He's always joking around. And didn't Joanne say that he was supposed to practice that Thursday? The queen has to be Sky! The poet even called her "Princess" in one line. That was Sky's costume at the dance, and she always calls herself "The Princess of Prescott." So Sky had something to do with what happened to Brandon. I knew it! But the poem said that the princess called the shots. That means Sky told someone else what to do. Who? "Fearful number in the night?" Who's the number? "Twenty minus four?" That's 16. Stephen. Stephen is number 16.

Someone saw what happened to Brandon. The person didn't want to tell, so he or she slipped this riddle in Tiffany's locker as a clue. What else could we do? We went to Principal Williams first thing this morning, showed him the poem, and told him our suspicions. I honestly thought that he'd take one look at the poem and dial 911. But you know what he said? He said, "Girls, this is hearsay. We don't have an eyewitness." He said, "That poem doesn't prove anything. Anyone could have written it as a joke, and vague allusions to queens and numbers don't amount to a hill of beans." He suggested that we keep our "fantasies" to ourselves because this is the sort of thing that starts rumors. Then he told us he was busy and sent us out the door.

I couldn't believe it. It's like he didn't even stop for one second to consider that we might be on to something. "Hearsay." "Fantasies." I've never been so insulted in my life. He acted as if we were a couple of little busybodies out trying to stir up trouble. I told Mom what happened. Tomorrow after school, she's taking us to the police department to talk to the detective who's investigating Brandon's case.

Wednesday
November 27
Joanne

We got out of school early today for the Thanksgiving holiday. Sage's mom took Sage, Tiffany, and me to the police station. This was the first time I've ever met Sage's mom. I thought she was going to be a real nut from the things Sage said at school. But she seemed just like other moms to me. She was actually quiet and kind of shy. Weird. Wonder why Sage thinks she's such a case.

We went to the police station because Tiffany and Sage are convinced that Sky and Stephen are responsible for what happened to Brandon. They had a riddle that Tiffany found in her locker. Whoever wrote it sure wanted to point the finger at those two. Tiffany and Sage insisted I go along so I could tell the police that Sky was late to practice that day.

The policeman in charge was super-nice. Sage knew him. He was the very same guy that accidentally hit Brandy on Halloween. How's that for small-town coincidence? He asked us a lot of questions about Brandon, Sky, and Stephen. I told him that Sky and Brandon didn't get along, but I didn't think she would go so far as to beat him half to death. She was late to practice that day, but then she's always late for everything, so that doesn't really mean much. Tiffany said that she'd heard Sky threaten Brandon just a couple of days before. Something about a Slo Poke being stuck to her skirt.

I don't know. Sky is terribly petty, and she can be really hateful, but I just can't believe she could have seen Brandon beaten like that and then come to practice like nothing had happened. Maybe whoever left the note doesn't like Sky and Stephen and is trying to get them in trouble. Maybe the poet is guilty, and that's why he or she is accusing someone else. I just don't want to jump to the conclusion that Sky was involved. We were friends for a long time.

I don't know what will come of us going to the police. Mr. Evans, that's the policeman, wrote a bunch of stuff on a legal pad, took the note Tiffany had found, and thanked us for coming. On the way out he talked to Sage's mom, but not about Brandon. He was asking about Brandy. He said he wanted to stop by and visit her again sometime. Like I said, he was really nice.

chapter 5

December

Upset all around

Borders drifting

Change profound

Power shifting

Courage found.

Subjects restless

Time for change

Witless mistress

Losing range.

Doesn't know it

Doesn't see

Why?

She is empty.

Joshua

Monday
December 2
Sky

So what? I hinted to Stephen that I'd like to see Brandon get his butt kicked. Does that make me guilty? I never touched Brandon. Not once.

Last Friday, the police called Daddy and told him that he had to bring me to the station to "answer a few questions." The Friday after Thanksgiving! Can you believe that? The nerve of some people. I really didn't have a clue what they could want to ask me. I thought maybe someone had finally found my gold bracelet that I had lost at the football stadium last year and maybe the police just wanted me to come identify it.

When we got to the station, they took Daddy and me into a little room. There were two policemen sitting at a table. They acted all nice, at first. But they were trying to trick me. Lucky I had Daddy there. Having an attorney in the family sure comes in handy when you're dealing with the likes of those guys. They asked me where I went after school on Thursday, November 14th. Honestly, am I expected to remember details about a day three weeks ago? I know that I go to practice every Thursday, but I wasn't sure which Thursday was the 14th, so I had no idea whose house I'd been to. When they told me that the 14th was the day Brandon was attacked, I remembered that I'd gone to Courtney's. How could I forget? That was the only time I had fun at practice all year. Brandon wasn't there hogging the whole show and bossing everyone around.

As I was saying, the police tried to trick me. They asked me what time I went to Courtney's. I told them that practice starts at 4:00. The ugly one with the big wart on his nose said, "We didn't ask you what time practice started. We asked you what time you got there." For God's sake! Do they think I carry a day planner around and jot down my every move? How was I supposed to know? Then they wanted me to tell them every single thing I had done from the time school let out until I got to Courtney's. Let's see. I went to the bathroom. Did they want to know whether I went number one or number two? Ugly didn't appreciate my humor. Daddy told me to quit being flippant and answer the "gentleman's" question. Whose side was he on, anyway?

So I told them that I left class, went to the bathroom, and walked to Courtney's. The nice policeman asked me how far it was to Courtney's from the school. Once again. "How am I supposed to know? I don't have an odometer taped to my ankle." That's when the nice cop became the bad cop.

He said, "Young lady, Courtney Harris lives five blocks from the junior high. You were released from school at 3:30. We have written statements from the other girls and Courtney's mother that you didn't arrive at practice until 4:30. How do you account for all that time?"

"Well, I said I went to the bathroom. I had to freshen my makeup. That takes a few minutes. Maybe I stopped to talk to friends. I just don't know."

"Did you talk to Stephen Johnson?"

"No, I never saw Stephen that day."

That's when I blew it. Evidently, the police had already been snooping around asking questions. One of the teachers told them that she "distinctly remembered" seeing me walk out of the gate with Stephen that day. I'll bet it was The Tank. She's too disgusting to have a life, so she has to get in mine. Or it could have been Laughinghouse. She's always trying to be the Good Samaritan. Anyway, they had me. I had to spill the beans. I'd tried to protect Stephen, but it was time for the truth to come out. I simply dissolved in tears. It was such a hard story to tell.

I told them how Brandon had hurt my feelings the day before by sticking candy on my chair. That when it got all over my new skirt, I became very upset. I mean, it wasn't just any old skirt. Momma had paid over $100 for it on sale. So in my anger, I told Stephen that I wanted to see Brandon "get his." Then the next day after school, Stephen and some of the other guys from the team asked me to walk out behind the school with them. Stephen said that they were going to catch Brandon on his way through the field and "teach him a lesson." I tried to talk them out of it. In fact, I followed them all the way to the edge of the field begging Stephen to change his mind. I told him that I wasn't worth it. That he'd get in trouble. And I told them that violence was not the way to solve problems. But they wouldn't listen. They waited for Brandon. He was coming through the field when Stephen ran up to him and shoved him down. Then the others started to hit and kick him over and over. I screamed and cried for them to stop, but they wouldn't. Brandon fought them for a while, but then he quit moving. That's when I ran away. I wanted to just die. I didn't know what to do, I was so upset. So I ran to Courtney's and tried to forget the whole thing. Honestly, I thought Brandon would be okay. In fact, I kept waiting for him to show up at practice. He had promised to show us some new stunts he'd learned in gymnastics, and I just couldn't wait for him to get there. But he never came.

I was crying so hard when I told the police what had happened, that I fainted, right there in the police station. Daddy brought me home.

Now we get a phone call, and they're going to make me go to a hearing at juvenile court. They want to charge me with aiding and abetting. Daddy says that they're just using scare tactics. He should know. I won't get in any trouble over this. I feel sad for Stephen, but he made his own bed. He and his friends will just have to pay for what they did.

Tuesday
December 3
Joanne

Stephen Johnson, Ricky Garza, Jeremy Dickson, and Patrick Webb were all arrested for beating Brandon. Who would have guessed? I see these guys every single day at school. They open doors for me and say hello when I pass them in the hall between classes. They seem like your average, normal kids. Then they go and do something horrible like put Brandon in the hospital. And Sky. What about her part in all of this? There's a rumor that Sky has to go to court with the boys next Wednesday. They're all back at school. Guess they don't lock kids up until the trial like they do adults. But none of them are talking. Stephen won't even look at Sky and vice versa. I saw them pass each other in the hall. Not a word. This is all so hard to believe.

Caras vemos, corazones no sabemons. "Faces we see, hearts we don't know." That about sums it up.

Wednesday
December 4
Tiffany

Everyone's so surprised that Stephen Johnson and three of his buds have been arrested for beating Brandon. I'm not. Joanne was shocked. She can't believe that people we go to school with every day can be so cruel. That's because Joanne is one of the beautiful people. When you're on her side of the fence, you don't see the same things the rest of us see. You haven't had chairs pulled out from under you and had to listen to everyone laugh while you're fighting back tears of pain and humiliation. You haven't had people draw ugly stick figures with buck teeth and bulging eyes on the chalkboard and scrawl your name underneath. You haven't been told to "sit someplace else," "join a different team," or "get out of the way." These are the things people have said and done to me since the first day of kindergarten.

For some kids like Joanne, school is a great place to be. People like you. They want to know what you're doing this weekend or where you bought your new shoes. For other kids, school bites. We try not to draw attention to ourselves. We sit in the back row, dart between classes, and eat alone. If someone does notice us, it's usually to find a new flaw or point out an old one that's worth a few more laughs.

No, I don't have any problem believing that kids can be cruel. What they did to Brandon was terrible. But kids tear down other kids every single school day. Maybe they don't send them to the hospital, but they make them sick with dread every weekday morning.

Grown-ups have it made. They're not stuck in a place where they're always on the outside. Mom says that school teaches us to get along with all kinds of people. She says that's a "good life lesson." Because grown-ups have to put up with all kinds of people that they don't like. Do they? If I were a grown-up, I would work someplace with people like me. In the grown-up world, nerds can be nerds in nice little cubicles next to other nerds, while they think of ways to patch the ozone layer. Freaks can get with other freaks to march for world peace. Beautiful people can live in beautiful houses in beautiful neighborhoods and socialize with other beautiful people. You can even be anonymous if you want; you can move to the city and live in a little apartment with a cat and a canary. Grown-ups can do whatever they want to get out of the way of people that hate them or people they hate. They can divorce, move, or quit their jobs.

But kids have to go to school and face every type of personality you can imagine, every weekday from August until May. We can't quit, we can't hide, and as much as we'd like to, we can't only associate with the people that we like. Things have gotten better for me. I have friends now. It makes school bearable. But what about kids like Jerky Josh?

By the way, Josh stuck that poem about Sky and Stephen in my locker. I know, because I saw him doing his language arts assignment on that same blue notebook paper. That puts Josh in a whole new light. He's a poet. He may be weird and quirky on the outside, but on the inside, he has talent. Like Emily Dickinson. She was weird too. But she got to lock herself up in her house and write fantastic poetry. I'll bet Josh wishes he could do that. I wonder how many other kids I pass in the hall every day have secrets like that. Maybe there is a Beethoven or an Einstein walking around Prescott in high-water pants and bifocals. Who knows? The point is, you never know who a person really is if you just judge him or her from the outside.

Thursday
December 5
Sage

Another Thanksgiving has come and gone. This year was much better than last year. Last year, we didn't even have a Thanksgiving dinner. Mom was dating the disc jockey. He had a "gig" at some rundown place on the lake—a place called The Barn. The name fit. Mom dragged me and Brandy there so we could watch her boyfriend spin records for a bunch of deadbeats. Imagine having nothing better to do on Thanksgiving than sit around in a smoke-filled bar, drinking beer and playing dominos. We were the only kids in the place. It was horrible. We ate greasy hamburgers and played pinball all day, while Mom sat at a table up by the stage and acted all gaga over Romeo's ability to operate a turntable.

But as I said, this year was better. We had a real Thanksgiving dinner with turkey, dressing, cranberry sauce, and Brandy's favorite—fruit salad. We helped Mom cook all morning. The food was great. Mom worked extra hard to put on a happy face. It was good, but it still didn't seem like Thanksgiving. No one was in the living room watching football. I missed Dad.

I wonder if he and Carly ate at home or if they went to some cafeteria and had Thanksgiving buffet with all of the other childless couples. That would be depressing enough, but Carly's cooking would be even worse. Burnt turkey, runny cranberry sauce, and Stove Top stuffing. That's what Carly would make. She's a terrible cook. Probably because she isn't old enough to have learned how. She went right from her Betty Crocker Easy Bake Oven to the real thing.

We're back at school. Things here are strange. Everyone is whispering about the big scandal. Stephen and his friends have been suspended from athletics and Sky's prancing around with her nose in the air, not speaking to anyone. She acts like she's being victimized. The only friend she has left is Candice. Julia and Courtney have gone their own way. Even the kids that a week ago would have given their left arm to be Sky's friend give her dirty looks and whisper behind her back.

Almost everyone's convinced that Sky was in on the whole thing. I'm sure she was. Joanne can't believe it. I guess she was around Sky more than other people, so maybe she saw some good in her that the rest of us didn't. All I've ever known of Sky is the spoiled brat. The girl who cuts you off mid-sentence because she's so sure anything she has to say is more important. The girl that makes fun of poor kids because they don't wear name-brand clothes. The girl that made Tiffany cry that day in the cafeteria. That's the Sky I know. I have no problem picturing her at Brandon's beating. To Sky, Brandon's just some trailer trash from the wrong side of the tracks. He doesn't even rate as a human being.

MONDAY
DECEMBER 9
BRANDON

Life is good. I'm back at home. Mom's waiting on me hand and foot. I don't have to go to school until after Christmas, and I'm typing this journal on Courtney's laptop. Good old Courtney. Some of my fingers on my right hand are broken, but I'm left-handed, so it doesn't keep me from being able to write. Only, Courtney doesn't know that, so she let me use this cool computer. I loaded a bunch of music and games. Mom sees me in here goin' at it on the keyboard and thinks I'm doing homework. As I said, life is good.

Pop got a doctor's release to go back to work. He had a heart attack last year, so they made him quit his job at the toilet factory. That's where he worked. This place out on the highway that makes toilets. So anyway, now he's out lookin' for a new job. The doctor says he can work as long as it's not manual labor. He's been in a good mood. He's even been nice to me. On Thanksgiving, we watched football while Mom slaved away in the kitchen. I tried to get under Pop's skin. He was gettin' all in a lather, yelling at the players on TV. Telling them how to play, calling them idiots, cheering them on. So I start carrying on about how some cheerleader screwed up a stunt. I thought I'd at least get a "queer boy" out of that one. But, Pop didn't take the bait. He only had three beers on Thanksgiving. Maybe that's why I couldn't get him riled up.

I gotta go to court Wednesday. Somebody snitched on Stephen and Sky. Serves 'em right. I hope the judge plasters them in honey and sticks them in an ant bed. That ain't gonna happen, though. I bet nothing happens to them at all.

Tuesday
December 10
Sky

I'm just sick of the kids at Prescott. How dare they act like I'm a villain. Courtney and Julia won't even speak to me. Stephen won't look at me. And even the geeks and nerds think they have a right to put in their ten cents. You would think that these people would feel sorry for me instead of acting like I did something wrong. I am just as much a victim in all of this as Brandon McCormick. Do you think people are treating him like a leper? Of course not! He's the sad little poor boy that those bad old rich kids put in the hospital. Whatever! Just because my daddy has lots of money doesn't mean that I'm the bad guy.

I honestly tried to stop Stephen. Then I tried to protect him from the police, which is what got me into this mess in the first place. I'm the only person who's shown any loyalty in all of this. I can't believe Courtney and Julia. They wouldn't be anything without me. I let them hang around with me all those years, basking in my popularity, and this is how they repay me. I expected as much from Joanne. She'd already turned into a Benedict Arnold when she went out with John.

Well! They'll all be sorry after the hearing tomorrow. Daddy says that if I'm telling the truth, I have nothing to worry about. They'll all see how I've suffered. It was so painful for me to have to watch Stephen and his friends do what they did. And then to have to pretend I didn't know anything all of those weeks. I've decided that I'm going to have to tell the judge the whole truth, even though it'll hurt

Stephen. The whole truth is that not only did I keep quiet to protect Stephen, but I also did it because I was afraid. I'd seen what Stephen was capable of and I thought that if I told, he might do something horrible to me. He's sick. Had I only known that he was a criminal, I would never have dated him. It's better that I tell. Stephen should be put away. He could hurt someone else.

Thursday
December 12
Joanne

Yesterday, I went to the hearing. The prosecutor asked me to go because he thought he might need to call on me to testify about Sky being late to practice or about Sky's relationship with Brandon. I didn't end up having to say anything. Sky did a pretty good job of prosecuting herself without any help from anyone. John, Sage, and Tiffany wanted me to try to remember every detail so I could tell them later what had happened. I took notes.

There weren't many people in the courtroom. It wasn't a trial by jury or anything like you see on television. It was just Sky, the boys who were accused of beating Brandon, their families, and Sky's dad. Joshua Melton was there too. I couldn't for the life of me figure out why until later. Brandon and his mom and stepdad were there. Then there were a few other people I didn't know and me.

The bailiff called everyone to order, and the show began. The judge was a big gray-haired man. He wore those half-moon glasses that our librarian wears. He kept them halfway down his nose so that when he wanted to look through them to read something, he had to tilt his head back and hold the paper up above his chin. Whenever he wasn't reading, he was peering over the top of the rims. He reminded me a character from *Oliver Twist*.

The first person to take the stand was Stephen. The judge asked him what he had done after school on the 14th of November. Stephen told him everything. He said that he'd waited for Brandon in the field behind school. He told him that he hit Brandon first. That they had fought for a minute, just the two of them. Then when Stephen knocked Brandon down, the other boys joined in and kicked him. Stephen started to cry while he was telling his story. He said that he was sorry he'd done it. That he hadn't meant for it to go so far. Then the prosecutor asked Stephen if Sky had been there and what role, if any, she played in the beating. Stephen said that it was Sky who had asked him to do it in the first place. That she had been there. And that she had cheered them on while they kicked and hit Brandon. Sky started to jump up and say something, but her daddy grabbed her arm and pulled her back to her seat.

The other boys testified one after another. Their stories were the same as Stephen's. Then Sky took the stand. She put her hand on the Bible, looked the bailiff straight in the eye, and swore to tell the whole truth and nothing but. As she went into her story, I kept getting the eerie feeling that lighting would come out of the ceiling and strike her dead. I wrote all of it down word-for-word. It was so amazing, I didn't want to forget a thing.

Judge: "Sky Davis, what did you do on the afternoon of November 14th?"

Sky: "I went to cheerleading practice. I'm a cheerleader, Your Honor."

Judge: "Yes, but did you do anything before cheer practice?"

Sky: "I went to school."

Judge: "You've heard testimony that you were present when these boys assaulted Brandon McCormick. Do you deny that?"

Sky: "Well, yes and no."

Judge: "Yes or no. Which is it?"

Sky: "Yes, I was there. But, no, it didn't happen the way they say it happened."

Judge: "Why don't you tell us how it happened."

Sky: "Okay, let me try to remember. Hmm. I left my last class and went to the bathroom to freshen my makeup. A girl should always look as fresh as the morning. Even for cheerleading practice. As I was saying, I freshened my makeup and left the bathroom. I was walking across the courtyard when Stephen stopped me. He told me that he wanted me to walk with him out behind the school.

"Well, now, Your Honor, I'm not the type of girl to go traipsing off to private places with some boy, even if he is my boyfriend. I told him no. That's when he threatened me. He told me that if I didn't come with him, something bad would happen to my friend Brandon. I was scared. Brandon is the leader of our cheer squad, and I knew that Stephen had it in for him. So I had no choice. Even if Stephen intended to violate me, I had to risk my own safety to save my captain. I went with him.

"There were some other boys behind the school. Those boys there." (She pointed at Ricky, Patrick, and Jeremy). "They said that they wanted me to walk out to the edge of the field with them, that they were going to catch Brandon McCormick and 'kick his . . .' I can't say that word, Your Honor. I turned on Stephen. I told him that he'd promised he wouldn't hurt Brandon if I came with him. He told me to 'shut up' and come with him or I'd get it too. I started crying. Stephen was supposed to be my boyfriend. I swear, Your Honor, I didn't know that he was insane until that very moment.

"Stephen and his friends forced me to go with them. The whole time I was begging for them not to do what they'd planned. I told them that Brandon was just a poor boy from a bad family. That he couldn't help being the way he is. That he didn't deserve this. They wouldn't listen. When Brandon came across the field, they attacked him. I screamed over and over for them to stop, but they wouldn't.

Then Brandon quit moving. It was horrible. Stephen turned to me, his fists scraped and bleeding. He looked just like Jack Nicholson in *The Shining*. He said to me, 'Sky, if you breathe one word of this, you'll be next. Only, you'll get it worse.' Being a girl and all, I can only imagine what horrors those monsters could inflict on me. Oh, Your Honor, I was just beside myself with fear. That's why I ran away and didn't tell anyone. I prayed all the way to Courtney's that Brandon would be okay. Then when I got there, I just forgot the whole thing. What else could I do?"

During her testimony, Sky kept dabbing at her eyes with a handkerchief that she just happened to have in her pocket. Her mother leaned against her dad and cried, sometimes rather loudly. The boys sat there with their mouths hanging open, like they were watching a stock-car race.

When it was over, the judge asked if the prosecutor had any questions. He said, no, Sky was free to step down. She couldn't hide the triumph in her face. She believed she'd won.

Then the prosecutor called Josh Melton to the stand. Poor Josh. He looked terrified. He walked forward, stiff as a board. The bailiff held the Bible out for him. Josh took it and turned it to face him, then handed it back to the bailiff. (He's so weird about everything being in a certain order). The judge asked Josh where he'd been the afternoon of the 14th. Josh said, "Behind the school."

"Where behind the school?"

"Behind a tree."

"Why?"

"I was thinking."

"Did you see anything unusual that afternoon?"

"I saw her. The princess."

"What was she doing?"

"She was telling Stephen to hurt Brandon."

"Are you sure?"

"Yes."

"What exactly did she say?"

"She said, 'You promised he'd get his. Now's your chance. If you're a real man, prove it. If not, we're finished.' "

"Then what happened?"

"The princess watched them hit Brandon."

"Did she try to stop them?"

"No."

"What did she do while they were hitting Brandon?"

"Cheers."

"Pardon me?"

"Cheers. Two bits, four bits."

"Thank you. You may step down."

That's when Sky jumped out of her seat. She said, "Your Honor, are you going to take the testimony of a retard?" The judge told her to sit down immediately. But she didn't listen. She said, "Your Honor, my daddy is an attorney. If you even consider this idiot's testimony, we'll take YOU to a higher court." That did it. The judge told Sky to get quiet or she'd be fined for contempt. Her dad looked so embarrassed. He pulled Sky down so hard I could hear her butt hit the seat.

The judge told everyone to take a break and come back in an hour. I heard Sky's mom really giving it to her dad on the way out. She asked, "Why don't you do something? Are you going to just sit there and let all of those boys lie about our baby?" He told her, "Our baby is a lying, conniving little brat." Then he walked off to the water cooler and left Sky and her mom standing there looking as if they'd just been punched in the stomach.

I went across the street to El Flamenco and killed an hour eating nachos. Then I went back for the grand finale. Everyone was already in the courtroom when I got there. We waited about five minutes before the judge came out. He peered over his glasses and cleared his throat. I could feel a speech coming on. He began by chastising Stephen and the other guys for what they'd done. He said that he was glad they showed remorse, but that wasn't enough. They would have to pay fines and restitution, and they'd have to do 40 hours each of community service with the Parks Department picking up trash, trimming trees, or whatever their supervisor directed them to do.

At this point, Sky was looking pretty smug. She thought she'd gotten off scot-free. Then the judge turned to her. He said, "Young lady, you have committed perjury in this courtroom today. I do not for one minute believe your innocence in regard to the crime in question. Though you didn't actually commit violence, you instigated it, which, in this court's opinion, is just as bad. You will do 40 hours of community service at the local soup kitchen. Your service will be completed by December 31 of this year."

That's when Sky lost it. She jumped out of her seat and demanded, "When do you expect me to do this community service? I have school all next week, and then we have Christmas holiday." The judge told her that the soup kitchen was open every day over the holiday, so it would be a perfect time for her to do her service. Sky said, "Well, I'm sorry, but NO! I have already made plans for my holiday. Momma and I have tons of shopping to do. I just don't have time to stand around slopping food to a bunch of losers. I'm sorry, Judge, but you'll just have to think of something else. Give me a fine or something. Daddy has plenty of money. He'll pay it."

The judge was speechless for a minute. I thought he was going to blow a fuse. Then he cracked up laughing. Big, loud, guffaws of laughter, like Sky was the funniest thing he'd ever seen in his life. It took him a good five minutes to regain his composure. Then he said, "Little girl, you will do as you're told. If you do not, I will have you placed in juvenile detention. Case closed."

Monday
December 16
Tiffany

This Wednesday, we get out of school for Christmas vacation. I can't wait. Joanne has invited me and Sage to go to New Mexico snow skiing. I've never been to New Mexico. In fact, I've never even been out of this state or seen snow. At first, I wasn't sure if I should go for a couple of reasons: I wasn't sure if Joanne really wanted me along, and I didn't think that I should leave Mom and Dad childless on Christmas.

I didn't think that Joanne really wanted me to go because she asked me at the same time she asked Sage. We were all sitting in the cafeteria together. I thought she asked me just because she'd brought it up and thought I might feel left out. But then, before I'd even gotten home from school, Joanne's mom called my mom and set the whole thing up. So I guess everything had already been worked out with Joanne's parents even before she asked me.

I'd worried all day that if I accepted the invitation, Mom and Dad would be bummed out about not having a kid around to open presents on Christmas morning. To tell you the truth, I've been secretly dreading Christmas. Last year was terrible. It was the first Christmas without Marilyn, and you just can't imagine what it's like to spend a holiday with someone so obviously missing. I tried to be extra jolly and do all the things Marilyn used to do, like make divinity and sing "Good King Wenceslas" while I hung up the stockings, but it was useless. I couldn't fill the void.

So I was totally relieved when I got home and Mom was going through my winter clothes to see what I had in the way of parkas and insulated socks. She was so excited about me going skiing with "the girls." A little too excited. It was like she and Dad couldn't wait to get me out of the house. Maybe being childless for a couple of weeks isn't the worst thing in the world for parents, even if it is over Christmas.

Miss Laughinghouse wanted us to write a final entry in our journals before the holiday and start it like this: If I could have anything in the world for Christmas, it would be . . . Okay, if I could have anything in the world for

Christmas, I would have friends, straight teeth, silky hair, and a snow skiing trip to New Mexico. I have the friends and the trip. What a start!

Tuesday
December 17
Sage

If I could have anything in the world for Christmas, I'd have my parents get remarried. But that isn't going to happen. I don't know, maybe I wouldn't have them get remarried. I wish they'd never gotten a divorce in the first place, but if they were to get remarried, that would be too weird—like resurrecting the dead. Mom and Dad have both changed so much that nothing would be the same if they did get back together.

Mom and I had a long talk the other night. She finally mentioned the journal. She apologized for "going temporarily insane." Then she talked to me about Dad. She told me that I shouldn't be so angry with him. I was surprised to hear her say that because, of course, if anyone has a reason to hate him, it's Mom. She told me that they had had a lot of problems before Dad got involved with Carly. That they'd started to "drift apart" several years ago, but because of us, they'd tried to pretend things were okay. She said Dad's affair hadn't really caused the divorce; it had just finalized something that had started to happen way back when.

I guess wishing them back together isn't what I'd really want. That would be too complicated. What would happen to Carly? How could they ever get over all the pain? No, it just wouldn't work. Besides, Brandy and I've already started to get over the whole ordeal. It's time to move on and let go of childish fantasies. Things actually aren't so bad. Mom's more like her old self, Brandy's cast is off, I have more free time for my friends, and our house is homey again like it used to be. I still miss Dad, especially at dinner. Sometimes, I catch myself turning toward his old place at the table to tell him something that happened at school. But I stop myself, and I don't get all sad about it like I used to, so I guess I'm getting better.

This isn't responding to Miss Laughinghouse's prompt very well. To be honest, I don't know what I could want for

Christmas that I don't already have. I get to go snow skiing with my friends. Who could ask for a better present than that?

Wednesday
December 18
Sky

If I could have anything in the world for Christmas, I'd take a one-way ticket out of this hick town. I'd go somewhere, probably Paris, where people can appreciate a girl like me. The problem with this town is that it's full of lowlifes, morons, and sexist pigs—that judge, for example. I know the only reason he found me guilty was because he has it in for beautiful girls. His wife is probably some dried-up old hag. So, like the fox in the fable, he hates beautiful women because he can't have one. I was no more guilty of what happened to Brandon McCormick than the man in the moon. But just because I'm a girl and I'm beautiful, that stupid judge nailed me. He wants to bring me down by sticking me in a soup kitchen with a bunch of do-gooders.

In my opinion, people who run around feeding the hungry and housing the homeless only do it because they can't get attention any other way. They're all ugly old women in tent dresses with outdated hairdos. And the men. They're the dorks you see running around in plaid pants and cardigan sweaters. Nope, if these people had lives of their own, they wouldn't feel compelled to go around getting into everyone else's. That judge was jealous of me. That's why he did this. He thinks that I'll become a dumpy do-gooder by osmosis. Then there'll be one less beautiful girl for him to look at and make him secretly loathe his miserable life with the crone.

Daddy is another example of a male chauvinist pig. I never thought I'd say that about my very own daddy, but it's true. These last few months, he's been limiting Momma on how much money she can spend. He set up a separate checking account for her and actually gives her an allowance. Can you believe that? An allowance. As if she's a little kid. Poor Momma can't possible live on the meager amount of money that Daddy's giving her. She bounced three checks last month. She can't even afford bare necessities. For example, the heel had broken off her mauve pumps. She had to replace them. What was she supposed to do? That was the only pair she had that matched her Gucci suit! So we went to the city and got a new pair. There was a terrific sale at Saks, so Momma picked up a few more things. She bought them on sale, for God's sake. You'd think Daddy would appreciate how frugal she's being. But, no! Her checks bounced, and Daddy threw a fit. He told Momma that if she didn't stop spending so much money, she was going to have to get a job! If that isn't being a male chauvinist, I don't know what is. A job! My mother's job is to stay at home and raise me. She keeps the house immaculate—with very little help from our lazy maid, Lupita; she cooks fabulous gourmet meals; and she always looks lovely when Daddy comes home from work. What more could a man possibly want?

chapter 6

January

So we begin another year
Vanquish pain and conquer fear
Forget an enemy, find a friend
Every beginning has an end.

Who is rich and who is poor?
Those with less sometimes have more.
Granite stone to sand can change
Time has the power to rearrange.

Joshua

Tuesday
January 7
Tiffany

The Christmas holiday was better than I could ever have imagined. We flew from the city all the way to Albuquerque, New Mexico. I had never been in an airplane before. At first, I was scared. But, Joanne, Sage, and I sat together way at the back of the plane, away from Joanne's parents. We had so much fun that I forgot I was a thousand miles off the ground. We took turns sitting by the window, talked about school, watched other people, listened to CDs, and daydreamed about what we'd do when we got where we were going.

From Albuquerque, we drove a rental car to Angel Fire. Everything was covered with snow. It was beautiful, like in a fairy tale. The lodge was way up in the mountains. It was built of logs just like the cabins in old John Wayne movies. It had a huge common room with massive stone fireplaces at either end. There were French doors that faced out onto a deck. You could lounge on the overstuffed couches and stare out over pine-covered mountains, sit at a table and play games, or snuggle up in a corner chair by the fireplace and read a book. I've never seen a place as fancy as that lodge, even in magazines.

Joanne, Sage, and I had our very own room. There were two queen-size beds and a bathroom with a tub so big you could almost swim in it. Joanne's parents had a room next to ours. At night, we came and went whenever we pleased, ordered pizza and sodas from room service, painted our toenails, and watched movies.

During the day we all went skiing. That is, they all went skiing. I had an accident the very first day. I was on the beginner slope, learning the ropes from this great-looking college student, when I lost my balance and went careening into a snow drift. I did something to my knee. So during the rest of the trip I stayed in the common room during the day while the others were out skiing. You would think that getting hurt and being stuck in the lodge would be the worst thing that could happen. But it wasn't. Something great happened. But I'm not going to say what—not yet. It's my secret. I want to keep it all to myself and savor it. I'm afraid if I talk about it, it'll lose some of its magic.

Anyway, when we got home, my parents were as happy as clams to see me. Not like they'd pined away for my company. Actually, they had a little honeymoon while I was gone. I was helping Mom clean house the day after I got back, and I found the evidence. Candle wax on the coffee table, take-out Chinese food cartons in the trash, and ticket stubs from *The Nutcracker*. Mom loves the ballet. Grandpa used to take her when she was a little kid, and she talks about it all the time. I guess Dad decided to treat her to something special this year. It paid off. Ever since I've been home, they're all kisses and hugs. To tell you the truth, they're so smoochy that it's embarrassing.

Thursday
January 9
Sky

This was absolutely the worst Christmas holiday I've ever had. I'll bet no one on God's green earth has ever had to put up with what I did over Christmas, and then I didn't even get one single thing I asked for from my "loving" parents. Honestly, if I had to spend one more Christmas like this one, I'd become Jewish just to avoid the holiday.

I spent four hours every weekday in the worst hell you can imagine. Our local soup kitchen is a nasty, rundown shanty over on the other side of the tracks. It's run by the African Methodist Evangelical Church. A whole congregation of do-gooders—just what the world needs. Every morning, Bertha (that's the soup kitchen cook) gets up and goes to that hole-in-the-wall to slop together a stew or some other God-awful concoction from donated food. There's no telling what goes into those big steaming pots. People clean out their cabinets every blue moon and pack over boxes of canned yams and Vienna sausages that they'd probably bought to stock their bomb shelters back during the Cold War. Hunters bring meat they don't want, and ranchers donate packages that contain parts of animals I wouldn't even want to mention.

It all goes into Bertha's giant cauldron. Bertha is a witch. I mean, really. She's huge and as ugly as the day is long. She has one gold tooth, and her hair's braided into all of these ropes that stick out from her head like that hideous lady from Greek mythology. I'll bet Bertha could turn people to stone, too, if she had a mind to. She's hateful. She raised her voice at me more than once. The very first day I told her that I simply could not wash dishes. I'd just had acrylic nails put on, and the hot water would ruin them. She yelled, "Git in der and wach dem dishes gil, fore I whack you wid dis spoon." Bertha is from Barbados. I'm sure that's where she learned the voodoo. She chants over the food. She says she's blessing it, but I'll bet she's cursing it. She probably wishes all of these beggars would drop dead so she wouldn't have to get up every morning and cook up their slop.

On my third day, when she told me to sweep the kitchen, I asked her where she'd parked her broom. That's the first time she gave me the evil eye. She throws her head back and looks at you with one eye half-closed, like she's sizing you up, but what she's really doing is putting a curse on you. I know because after she did it to me, I started feeling sick. I felt feverish that whole afternoon. I told her I was sick and needed to go home. She told me, "Da only ting you's sick of, gil, is wuk." She wouldn't even let me call Momma.

The same horrible people come into the soup kitchen every day. Toothless old men that stink to high heaven, women with scabby sores on their faces, and filthy snot-nosed kids. This one couple came every day and brought their baby. The baby cried constantly. It was enough to make me want to jump out of my skin. One day, Bertha walked over, picked that dirty baby up off the bench, and started singing some song in gibberish. The baby stopped crying and fell right to sleep. She'd cursed it. I didn't even bother to tell Momma what I'd seen—further proof of Bertha's voodoo. She wouldn't have believed me anyway. Ever since that judge called me a liar, my parents give each other this look whenever I try to tell them something important. For God's sake, what's this world coming to? A girl's own parents would rather believe a sexist pig than their daughter, a witch runs the local soup kitchen, and the most beautiful girl in this town is working like Cinderella to feed a bunch of lazy bums.

The worst day of the holiday was Christmas. I actually had to go to the soup kitchen and put in my four hours from eight until noon. It was horrible. Bertha had put up a ragged old artificial Christmas tree and decorated it with the tackiest ornaments you can possibly imagine. There wasn't one thing on that tree that coordinated with anything else. She had balls of every color, tinsel in gold and silver, and she'd even sprayed it with fake snow. The tree was almost as ugly as Bertha. Under it, there were about 30 packages wrapped in newspaper. Every time someone came in to eat, Bertha would pull a package from under the tree and give it to the poor sap. You'd think these people had never seen a pair of mittens or a scarf before, the way they carried on about the junk she gave them for Christmas. The kids were the worst. Bertha gave them Dollar Store toys, and they cradled them in their arms like the goose had laid a golden egg especially for them. Pathetic, I tell you. I just wanted to stand on a bench, bang some pot lids together, and scream, "Get a job!" to the whole motley crew. If they'd get off their butts and work, they could have a real Christmas with a real tree and some real presents. But I kept my mouth shut. I didn't want to get hexed by the voodoo queen and spend Christmas evening in bed with the heebie-jeebies.

Had I known how the rest of Christmas day would go, I probably would have gone ahead and told them all off, including Bertha. Even if she'd turned me to stone, Christmas couldn't have been any more horrible. I got home from the soup kitchen, all sweaty, my nails shot to hell, smelling like gruel and kerosene oil, and took a nice long bubble bath. The whole time I was soaking in the suds, I was daydreaming about the diamond earrings and all of the beautiful clothes I would be trying on in just a few hours. We were going to open gifts before supper. Well, I should have just slipped under the suds and drowned myself.

When I went into the living room, there weren't but two packages under the tree for me. "No cause for alarm. Probably diamonds," I told myself. But, guess what? I got a pair of sterling silver loop earrings, and a gift certificate for $50 to J.C. Penney. I honestly thought they were playing a joke. I said, "Daddy, come on now, where are you hiding my real presents?" He looked mad! He said, "Sky, it's time we had a little talk." Then he told me the biggest whopper you've ever heard. He said we were having financial problems: that we'd spent so much money on credit, we had more payments every month than he brought home in salary. He said that we had to start "cutting corners."

Momma was crying when he told me. I know he's lying. There is no way that we're going broke. Only people like Brandon McCormick and his trailer-park neighbors "go broke." Daddy's just trying to punish me for getting into trouble over Brandon. And he's mad at Momma because she doesn't want to live on an allowance. He's stingy, that's what he is. He's mad at us, so he wants to keep all of his money for himself. He said I was a "spoiled brat" at the courthouse that day. Well, he hasn't seen a spoiled brat yet.

Friday
January 10
Sage

I've decided that as soon as I graduate from college, I'm going to move to the mountains. I want to live someplace beautiful and secluded. It would be great. I could hike or ski during the day and cozy up with a good book every night. I'll have Brandy out to visit once a month. She can find all kinds of cool things to add to her collection. I brought her a huge pinecone that I found in the woods near the lodge. She was thrilled, even though half of it had gotten smashed in my suitcase on the flight home.

I'd worried about Brandy while I was gone. I was afraid that she wouldn't have a good Christmas without me. But she spent Christmas with Dad and Carly, and from the stories she told, it sounds like she didn't miss me all that much. They opened packages Christmas morning. Then they drove to the city and went to a diner for Christmas dinner. Not exactly your traditional Christmas, but Brandy's too little to be hung up on tradition anyway.

Mom spent Christmas alone. I hadn't even thought about what it would be like for her with both of us gone. She said it was nice. She spent the day cleaning out the attic and then in the evening, she read a book. Poor Mom, what a way to spend a holiday. Things picked up for her the next day, though. She went to the grocery store and ran into—guess who? Mr., or should I say, Sgt. Evans—the very same guy that hit Brandy with his car on Halloween and solved the mystery of the Brandon McCormick beating. Mom said that he was standing in front of a cooler trying to decide between brussel sprouts and French cut green beans. They got into a conversation, and before you know it, they left their grocery baskets full of groceries sitting in the frozen food section and took off for a restaurant.

Come to find out, Mr. Evans—Mike—had spent Christmas alone just like Mom. Only, he cleaned out his garage instead of his attic and chose football over Faulkner. He's never been married. Kind of strange for a guy that old, but, according to Mom, he never found the time to date much when he was in college. Then before he knew it, he was 40 and single, wondering where all the years had gone.

Mom said they sat in that restaurant from 6:00 in the evening until it closed. The next day, he took her to the lake for a picnic—in the middle of winter. Since then, they've been out twice. He's called every night since I've been home. Mom seems happy about it. Not silly happy, like with her other boyfriends. She doesn't go on and on about him or dress up in dumb teenager clothes. She's peaceful happy. She goes about her housework like she's on cloud nine, humming the theme song to

Titanic. Sometimes I have to tell her something three or four times before she even notices that I'm talking. I'll say, "Mom, do we have any mayonnaise?" She keeps on wiping the stovetop. "Mom, do we have any mayonnaise?" Still wiping. Then finally I say, "HEY, MOM!" She'll stop what she's doing, turn around, look at me with a vacant smile, and say, "Hmmm? Honey, did you say something?" Too weird.

Wednesday
January 15
Joanne

Tiffany has a secret. She acted strange on our ski trip, and she's still acting goofy. I haven't figured it out yet, but I have my suspicions. There was this boy at the lodge. I never saw him on the slopes, but he and his parents ate in the dining room almost every night. I wouldn't have even noticed him if I hadn't seen he and Tiffany giving each other secret looks when they thought no one was watching. When I asked Tiffany if she knew him, she blushed and changed the subject. Sage didn't notice a thing. She was too busy daydreaming about building a cabin in the woods. But I noticed. Tiffany has something up her sleeve.

It was good to get back home and see John, but other than that, I wish I was still in New Mexico. We're back at school. Brandon is all healed and clowning again. He and Courtney have something going. It's funny. Courtney and Brandon, who would have ever thought? Sky and Candice are still friends, but other than that, the old gang has dissolved into nothingness. Speaking of Sky, I saw her mother drop her off this morning. She was driving an old minivan. When Sky got out, she yelled across the parking lot to Candice, "Our Mercedes is in the shop. Doesn't that just bite?" She wanted everyone to hear. I suppose she was afraid that riding to school in a minivan might jeopardize her social status. Still the same old Sky.

FRIDAY
JANUARY 17
BRANDON

Back at school, and all is well. I'm an overnight hero. If I'd known that gettin' my butt kicked would make me a chick magnet, I'd have ticked off old Stephen Johnson years ago. I'm playing it for all it's worth. I hobble around like I'm in pain, and girls come outta the woodwork to carry my books and open doors for me. Courtney gets all bent, but she gets over it fast enough. All I gotta do is lay the ol' McCormick charm on her, and she's putty in my hands.

Pop got a job. He's selling cars up at the Dodge dealership. A used car salesman—perfect. Better than makin' toilets. He's already sold three cars, and he hasn't been there but a week. That's some kinda record according to his boss. Pop's a charmer like me. He could sell snowshoes to the devil—least that's what he says. His first customer was Sky Davis's mom. How 'bout that for irony, Laughinghouse? Yeah, looks like the Davises are coming down in the world. Traded in that kickin' Benz on a used minivan. Pop said Old

Lady Davis cried when she was handing over her keys "like she was givin' away her own kid or something." Come to think of it, if Sky's mom had a choice, she'd probably rather part with the kid than the car. I know I would.

Monday
January 20
Tiffany

I've decided to go ahead and reveal my secret. But only in this journal because I'm still afraid if I tell my friends, I'll jinx it somehow—that I'll tell everyone, and then Treiu will up and disappear like a figment of my imagination. Treiu is my boyfriend. There, I said it. I, Drucilla the buck-toothed, dirty dishwater kid, have a boyfriend. I still can't believe it. That's why I'm writing it down. The longer I keep it to myself, the less real it seems.

Anyway, this is how it happened. The day after I hurt my knee skiing—or rather, trying to ski—I went into the common room at the lodge to find a good book. They have a small library along one wall with leather-bound copies of all the classics. I grabbed *Moby Dick*, thinking that I'd read something really profound so I could tell my parents that I did something useful with my spare time. I snuggled up in the corner in a big, soft chair, and started applying myself to adventure on the high sea. But I just couldn't stay focused. Pretty soon, I was peeking over the top of my book, watching people come and go. That's when I saw Treiu for the first time. He was in the opposite corner, peeking over his book, watching me. He caught me watching him watch me. I was so embarrassed, I stuck my face back in *Moby Dick* as fast as I could. But it was too late. We'd made eye contact. How could I concentrate on ugly old Captain Ahab when there was a good-looking boy right across the room? I peeked around my book, and there he was, still looking at me. He got up and started walking over. I was so nervous, I thought I was going to be sick to my stomach. Wouldn't that have been cute? "Hi, my name's blaaaaaaah." I could see myself puking on his shoes. But he challenged me to a game of Scrabble, and before I knew it, we were telling each other our life stories.

Treiu is pronounced "true." *His* name fits him. He wasn't born in the United States. They moved to the States from Vietnam when he was five. Guess what? He lives 30 miles from here, in the city. What a coincidence. He likes old movies, board games, books, and Tiffany Andrews—*me*. He likes me! While my friends were out skiing, Treiu and I watched old movies on a VCR in the annex, played gin rummy and Scrabble, or just sat and talked about anything and everything. He has asthma, so he doesn't ski, and lucky for me, my knee never got well enough for me to leave the lodge. For two weeks we carried on a secret love affair.

When the others would come in for the evening, Treiu and I would go our separate ways and pretend we didn't know each other. I wanted it that way. I was afraid if Joanne and Sage knew, they'd joke around about it or say something to Treiu that would be embarrassing. Not on purpose, of course. Just something like, "Oh, you're Tiffany's boyfriend?" To tell the truth, Treiu and I never said "boyfriend" or "girlfriend" out loud to each other. That would have been mushy and uncomfortable. But I know he's my boyfriend because he held my hand while we watched *South Pacific*, and because he's written me four letters since I came home. He signs them, "Love, Treiu."

Thursday
January 23
Sky

Daddy is a tyrant! When faced with tyranny, one must take drastic measures. I'm starving myself. That's what that old guy from India did. If it worked for a little prune in bifocals, why shouldn't it work for me? Things are just dreadful at home. Daddy forced Momma to trade in our car on the ugliest old minivan you've ever seen. A minivan, for God's sake! Only geeks ride around in minivans. Oh, and if that wasn't bad enough, he fired Lupita. True, she wasn't the best maid ever—sometimes she forgot and put my jeans into the dryer, and of course, I wouldn't wear them again, so I'd have to buy new ones—but she did keep the house halfway decent. Now he expects *me* to do *her* job. Last night he told me to wash dishes. Can you believe it? I refused. I will *not* do menial labor in my own home. I went to my room and slammed the door. Momma washed the dishes. Poor Momma. Had she known that Daddy would go insane at 40, she probably would never have married him.

So now I'm going to starve myself until

Daddy comes to his senses, gets our car back, and hires another maid. He thinks he's fooling me with all of his talk about financial problems. We have money. We always have, and we always will. I think he's trying to get Momma to leave him. That's what I think. He's pretending he's broke so she'll file for divorce. He turned 40 last month, and you know what they say about the 40-year itch. My Uncle Nigel got it, and he ran off with a nightclub dancer. Daddy and Nigel are brothers. There must be some genetic insanity that kicks in when their hair starts turning gray.

To make matters worse, the kids at school have all gone crazy too. They're kissing up to Brandon McCormick like he's a prince. Some prince! If they'd seen him balled up on the ground getting kicked in the head, they wouldn't think so highly of him. What a loser! Candice is the only person at school who still has her wits about her. She's agreed to starve herself right along with me. I can't do this alone. When Candice and I start to turn to skin and bone, they'll all see what they've done, and the world will be set right again. Then I'll have Momma drive the Mercedes to Dairy Queen, pick me up a cheeseburger and a diet Coke, come home, eat it at the kitchen island, leave a big mess for the new maid, and go to bed happy.

Tuesday
January 28
Sage

It's been a whole month, and Mom's still dating Mike. He came over last Friday for dinner. It was nice. He didn't try to shoo me and Brandy out of the room like Mom's other boyfriends, and he left when it was time for us to go to bed. Mom's quiet around Mike. Not shy-quiet, or bored-quiet, just happy-quiet. She doesn't seem to be trying so hard to make him like her, the way she did with the others. When he was at the house, it was almost like having Dad back. Not that Mike's anything like my dad. It's just that he isn't imposing. He fits in. Brandy likes him too. She thinks it's just the coolest thing that he's a policeman. Little kids are fascinated by that sort of thing.

7

chapter

February

Heart of gold to be rewarded
Evil mind, view distorted
One who loves to find a friend
While hateful one seeks bitter end.

Joshua

Thursday
February 4
Joanne

Tomorrow is Sage's thirteenth birthday. I turned 13 last June. It wasn't nearly as special as I thought it would be. You think, okay, I'm finally leaving childhood behind and becoming a real, bonafide teenager. You'd think you'd feel different, but you don't. You're still the same kid you were the day before, only now people think every time you're in a bad mood that it has something to do with hormones. And that's only one of the annoying things about becoming a teenager. Another annoying thing is that your parents get more uptight when you talk about boys. If I talked about boys when I was in the fifth grade, Mama would just smile and say, "How cute." Now when I talk about John, she asks a hundred questions like: "Does John do well in school?" "Has he ever been in any kind of trouble?" "What do his parents do for a living?" I get a regular inquisition whenever I bring up his name.

But I don't suppose Sage will have problems talking to her mom about boys because Sage isn't even interested in having a boyfriend. She has her whole life planned from graduation to old age. She's decided to be a forest ranger. She got the idea last week when we watched a documentary in science class. Sage knows everything she wants to do with her life, even down to the kind of house she's going to live in. But she never mentions a husband or kids as part of her plan. Oh well, like Grandma says, *Cada perico a su estaca, cada changa a su mecate.* "To each his own."

We're getting together at Sage's Friday night for a sleepover to celebrate the big day. I had no idea what to buy her for a birthday present. What do you get for a girl like Sage? She doesn't wear makeup, has hair too short to put up in a clip or ponytail, and couldn't really care less what she wears to school. I instant-messaged John and Tiffany, and we decided to pool our money and buy her a telescope. John actually pitched in more than the rest of us. He mowed lawns all last summer and still hasn't spent all of the money he made. John isn't like anyone else our age. I would have spent that money the first week. But he's always planning ahead. That's why he and Sage are such good friends. They think alike.

Monday
February 10
Tiffany

I went to Sage's house last Friday for her birthday party. It was great. John's dad had taken him to the city to get her present. We all pitched in and bought her a telescope. I only had $20 to spend. I think John must have put in way more than his share, because the telescope was huge. We set it up in the backyard and looked at the moon. There are all kinds of adjustments that you can make to get a better view, but none of us really knew what we were doing, so we couldn't get a good look at any stars. Just the moon. When you look at the moon up close, it's like a big, grinning face—a cynical, old fat man laughing at us. Creepy!

This coming Friday is the school Valentine dance. Valentine's Day used to be my least favorite holiday. I hated it. Especially when I was in grade school and the teachers made us exchange cards with our classmates. Mom would buy a huge box of Valentine cards, and I'd fill in a card for everyone in my class. It took me forever because first I'd have to sort through the cards and throw out all the sappy ones. I didn't want to give some kid a card that said, "You're my one and only Valentine" or "Be mine." What if they thought I really meant it? Then the kids would tease me.

Actually, I only took cards one year. After that, to save myself the agony of possibly screwing up and getting a sappy card mixed in with the others, I'd address them at the dining room table so Mom would see me. Then the next day, I'd throw them in the trash as soon as I got to school. I'd tell the teacher I'd forgotten to bring them. In the third grade, my teacher wouldn't let me be part of the Valentine party because I hadn't brought the stupid cards. So while all the other kids were having cupcakes and punch, I had to sit in the hall and copy definitions out of the back of our spelling book. Like I said, Valentine's Day was my least favorite holiday. This year is different. I have a Valentine of my very own. Treiu wrote me twice last week.

Wednesday
February 12
Sky

Starving myself isn't as easy as I'd thought it would be. Momma makes me a salad every morning to take to school. But I don't eat it—well, not all of it, at least. I only eat half. I don't have any supper. I sit at the dinner table with Momma and Daddy and refuse even to put any food on my plate. Momma is so worried. Daddy doesn't care one bit. He says, "She'll eat when she gets hungry enough." He probably wouldn't care if I dropped dead right there at the table with my face in my empty plate. I can just see him looking at Momma and saying, "Well, there's one less mouth to feed."

Candice is cheating. I can tell. She doesn't look like she's lost one single pound, and we're supposed to have been starving ourselves for over a week now. Yesterday, I thought I saw a package of Skittles when she opened her backpack to get her brush. Well, that's just par for the course! I should have known that I couldn't trust anyone to suffer with me. That Gandhi had to go it alone too. You didn't see any of his buddies lying next to him on his cot wasting away along with him. Just him, alone, suffering to free everyone else.

I told Candice how selfish it was for her to expect me to do this all by myself. She said, "Well, Sky, why should I starve so you can get your car back?" That's how simple she is. She thinks this is all about a car and a maid. It's much bigger than that. I'm starving myself to free all women from oppressive men. Men like Daddy and that judge who think they can up and call the shots any old time just because they wear the pants.

This Friday is the Valentine dance. And I don't have one single thing to wear. I told Momma that I had to have a new dress, and do you know what she said? "Wear one of your old ones, Sky." Daddy's finally gotten to her. Momma's been brainwashed.

Or maybe there's another explanation for the way things are going. I thought of this last night. I was tossing and turning, dreaming of cheesecake, when it came to me. I remembered something. We've been cursed by Bertha. One day in the soup kitchen, this little kid spilled hot stew all over my new Adidas shoes then had the nerve to ask for a second helping. I told that kid that he could go home hungry and next time he'd be more careful with what he had. Bertha came out of the back and brought the kid another bowl. Then she turned around and gave me the evil eye. I didn't get sick or anything. So I thought maybe the curse hadn't worked. But look at us now. I'm hungry, Momma has to wash dishes, and Daddy's turned into an evil dictator. It's the soup kitchen all over again!

Thursday
February 13
Sage

It's been a while since I've written in this journal. I don't really think it matters if I keep up every single week. Miss Laughinghouse passes everyone, no matter what they do. I think she's afraid that if she doesn't, she'll damage someone's self-esteem. The kids are all onto her. So students do even less in her class than they did at the beginning of the year. I feel sorry for her sometimes. Kids don't listen to her at all. You can tell she really wants to be a good teacher, but no one can hear her over all the talking and playing around.

My birthday was the best ever. John, Joanne, and Tiffany came over. They gave me a telescope. It's awesome. I'll keep it forever. When I'm a ranger, I'll put it up in the tower and stare at the stars while I'm waiting for a forest fire or some other calamity. It was the perfect gift. After we played with the telescope, we roasted hot dogs over a fire in the backyard pit. Then we told ghost stories until John had to go home. You'd think that in all the time Tiffany, Joanne, and I sat talking before we finally fell asleep, that Tiffany would have let us in on her secret. But it wasn't until the dance Friday night that we found out why she's been so giddy lately. What a surprise, Tiffany has a boyfriend.

MONDAY
FEBRUARY 17
BRANDON

Friday was Valentine's Day. I started back to work at the theater two weeks ago, so I had some extra cash to burn. I got Mom a dozen red roses. She started bawlin' and carrying on over it. She hugged me and told me I was a great kid and all that crap. Kinda made me wish I'd a gotten her somethin' a little less sappy, like a blender. Women are strange. Courtney, for example. I got her one of those fancy flower things you wear on your wrist and took her to the Valentine dance and out for pizza. But you think all that would make her happy? Heck, no! She didn't say two words to me the whole night, just 'cause I danced with some other girl. I tried to explain how things work. "A guy like me can't be owned by just one babe. When you got it all, you got to share the wealth with those less fortunate." Now she won't answer my phone calls or talk to me at school. I told Pop what happened, hoping he'd give me some manly words of wisdom. He just said, "Women!" Course I shoulda known not to ask for advice on romance from a guy who bought his wife a new spare tire for Valentine's.

Monday
February 17
Tiffany

Valentine's Day is now my favorite holiday. I went to the dance last Friday night with Joanne, John, and Sage. I almost begged off and stayed home to read. Thank God I didn't. We went at 7:00. Most everyone was already there. They gym was decorated in big, glittery red hearts, and the DJ played one love song after another. I was having fun, but I couldn't help thinking about Treiu. I finally had a boyfriend, and I didn't even get to see him. I was feeling kind of sorry for myself.

Anyway, Joanne, John, Sage, and I were all out on the dance floor dancing to a fast song when I glanced toward the door and saw Treiu. I almost fell over. I had to blink really hard to make sure I wasn't seeing things. But there he was, watching me, just like that first time at the lodge. I didn't know what to do. Should I run toward him and risk tripping in my heels, or should I just keep dancing and wait for him to come to me? I didn't do either. Before I could get to him, Principal Williams stopped him and started giving him the third degree. Kids who don't go to Prescott aren't allowed at the dances. Treiu charmed Williams into letting him stay. After all, his parents had already dropped him off and left to go to a restaurant. What could he do?

We had the best time. All the kids at the dance kept looking at us. I'll bet they were really surprised to see the buck-tooth, dirty dishwater kid with a date. Sage and Joanne were totally shocked. Joanne said that she'd suspected all along, but she still couldn't stop jabbering on about "my secret." At first, I was insulted that they thought it was so amazing for me to have a boyfriend. But then I figured out it wasn't that I had a boyfriend that they found so incredible, it's that I'd kept it a secret all this time. They think I'm strange because I don't volunteer information about every detail. That's me. I'm a mystery.

Tuesday
February 18
Joanne

Tiffany is something else. She had a boyfriend for two whole months and didn't even tell her closest friends. But that's Tiffany.

She keeps her business to herself. I, personally, can't keep a secret for more than a day. Well, I can, but only if it means life or death to someone else. Tiffany likes to sit on things and think them over before she opens her mouth. I wish I was more like her in that way. Instead, I just blurt out whatever I'm thinking, and then I regret it afterward.

Like today, I stuck my foot in my mouth twice. First, I made Miss Laughinghouse cry. I didn't mean to. Everyone was talking, and this boy that sits next to me was throwing M&Ms across the room to his friend. I was trying to do my work, but I had to read the same sentence four times because I couldn't think with all the commotion going on around me. I told Miss Laughinghouse that she needed to do something. She stopped mid-sentence and started to crumble right in front of us. Before I knew what was happening, she was at her desk with her face in her hands, crying. I really didn't mean to hurt her feelings. It isn't her fault that the kids won't listen. She just isn't mean enough, that's all. How can you fault a person for that?

Then later in Spanish class I thought I'd say something nice to Sky. Just to try and make peace. Not that I want to be her friend again, but I feel sorry for her. Most people would think that's crazy. Sky brought misery on herself. But she was my friend once, and lately she's been looking really burned out. She's lost weight, her hair's dried up, and she has big dark circles under her eyes. So I said, "Hey, Sky, are you feeling okay? You don't look so good." Boy, she just about bit my head off. She thought I was insulting her, when all I really wanted to do was show concern for an old friend. She said, "I don't look so good? *I don't look so good*? How should a person look when she's suffering for humanity? Like a model, Joanne? Like a movie star?" I was speechless. What was she talking about? Suffering for humanity? Sky? I hate to say this, but I think she's starting to lose her mind. Probably what she did to Brandon is eating at her conscience.

Friday
February 21
Sky

I'm sick with hunger, and nobody cares. Our car is probably gone by now, but it doesn't matter. I won't eat until Daddy sees things my way. I think I may be dying. I'm so tired all the time that it's just about all I can do to come home from school and drop into bed. I didn't even go to the Valentine dance. What fun is a dance, anyway, when you don't have anything new to wear?

I can't seem to keep my thoughts straight. Sometimes, I'll be in class listening to Mrs. Clark ramble on about Vietnam and I start thinking I'm there, right on the front lines, being shot at by someone named Charlie. The other day the kid in front of me dropped his book on the floor during one of Mrs. Clark's stories. The sudden bang shocked me so badly that before I could stop myself, I'd thrown my arms over my head and yelled, "I surrender." Everyone thought it was a joke. Mrs. Clark gave me detention. My mind's slipping. This morning, I almost left the house in my slippers. Can you believe it? I can just see myself climbing out of that ugly minivan in fuzzy pink house shoes. I'm living a nightmare.

8

chapter

MARCH

Call her mental
Call her insane
Is she crazy?
Or is she just vain?

She takes from others
To serve her plot
She doles out pain
Without a thought.

Joshua

Monday
March 2
Sage

Great news! Mike bought a house at the lake. He and Mom went to their old picnic spot last weekend, and while they were driving home they came across this place for sale. Mom says that it's right on the lake and surrounded by woods. The house needs a lot of work. But who cares?

I really like Mike. Not just because he has a lake house either, though I have to admit that's a definite perk when it comes to potential stepfathers. I like him because he treats Mom nice and because he doesn't act like it's a pain having Brandy and me around. Oh, and he knows a lot about telescopes. He showed me how to adjust mine so that I can see Orion. I'm going to take it to the lake with us over spring break. I'll bet I can see for miles without all the light pollution. That's city lights that interfere with seeing the stars. Mike taught me that.

Friday
March 7
Sky

Life just can't get any worse. I came home from school yesterday to find a couple of fat middle-aged strangers walking through my house. Some snooty lady with a big, outdated hairdo was showing them the inside of our cabinets, for God's sake, just like it was her house. When I got over the shock and found words, I asked her just what the hell she thought she was doing. That's when Momma came in from the living room and pulled me aside to let me know that she and Daddy had decided to sell our house and buy something "a little more affordable." I fainted right then and there.

When I came to, I was lying on the couch with a cold rag on my head. At first, I thought the whole thing had just been one of the nasty nightmares I'd been having, but then the real estate lady came sidling up to me with a glass of ice water. At least those hideous toads that had been rummaging through our cabinets had the decency to leave before I had to see them again. Imagine, fat people living in OUR house, swimming in OUR pool. I told that ugly hairdo real estate lady that she wasn't getting her nasty paws on our house to turn a fast buck. Momma and Daddy have gone temporarily insane, and when they come around, which will be in short order, believe you me, they will ditch this whole insane idea and get back to living like we always have. I screamed at her, "Get out of my house, NOW." She left, thank God, right before I fainted again.

Last night at dinner, Daddy started in on me about not eating. I told him point blank that until he stopped selling our stuff and acting like a pauper, I wouldn't touch another bite. I meant it too. Even though I'm so weak I can hardly make it through the day, I won't give up until Daddy stops this nonsense. I'll die before I move into some little brick house in a middle-class neighborhood. I deserve so much more.

Monday
March 17
Sage

I had more fun this spring break than I've ever had in my entire life. We left the house Friday evening around 7:00 to head for the lake. I wanted to leave as soon as we got home from school, but Mom was still packing and checking over her list. She had to run to the grocery store for: sunscreen, bug spray, cough medicine, nasal decongestant, Tylenol, an emergency bee sting kit, and everything else she could think of that a person would need on a three-month safari in Africa. Sometimes she really overdoes it.

From the minute I came home from school until we left, I could do nothing but pace. I'd been packed since Wednesday. I hate to wait. We finally left. Mom, Brandy, Tiffany, Joanne, and me. All crammed into our little Mazda. The whole gang chatted and laughed on the way. Not me. I couldn't think about anything but where we were going. What would it be like? I had no idea. Mom wouldn't tell me anything about the lake house, no matter how much I begged her. The anticipation was killing me.

We drove halfway around the lake before Mom slowed down and pulled into a long, narrow, dirt driveway lined with flowering shrubs. I kept trying to see over Brandy's head to find the house, but it didn't come into view until the drive turned to the left. There it was. The most beautiful house I'd ever laid eyes on. Sure, it needed a little work. The shutters were hanging cockeyed on several windows, the paint was peeling, and the screens were ripped and sagging, but it was beautiful all the same. I almost tripped over Tiffany on the way to the back door. I couldn't wait to get inside that house and see what treasures it held. We went in through the back door. It opens onto a screened porch that was literally crammed full of old junk. Mike had bought the house "as is," which meant he got to keep all of the cool stuff previous owners had left behind. What a great deal!

We had to move some junk to get to the kitchen door. When we finally got it open and Mom switched on the light, my mouth fell open. Mom put her arm around me and said, "A little elbow grease, and it'll come around, Sage. You'll see." She misunderstood my awe. The kitchen was fabulous. The refrigerator was one of those really old ones with rounded edges. All of the cabinets up top had wooden doors, and the ones down below had tattered blue-and-white checked material hung like curtains to hide the stuff inside. In the middle of the kitchen was a Formica table with red chairs. It was the cutest kitchen on earth.

Between the kitchen and the living room, there was a pocket door that slid right out of the wall. In the living room there was a huge old couch and two chairs with ottomans, a fireplace, and windows that reached almost from the floor to the ceiling. Brandy plopped down onto one of the chairs, and a cloud of dust billowed up, throwing her into a coughing spasm. The room stretched from one side of the house all the way to the other. Behind it and alongside the kitchen was Mike's bedroom. It already looked like it belonged to a man. The first thing I saw when I walked through the door was a big fish mounted on a plaque over a massive old dresser.

I was just wondering where we were all going to sleep when Mom walked back out of Mike's room into a tiny hall and opened a door. There were stairs. Rickety, narrow stairs. We followed her up single-file. I was last. I wanted to shove everyone out of the way and get in front. I was dying to know what was at the top of those stairs. It was worth the wait. Our room, mine and Brandy's, was the coolest room in the house. It was huge. The room sat under the roof, so the ceiling came down almost to the floor on two walls. The other two walls were like big triangles with little shuttered windows right in the middle. Twin beds sat on either side of the window on one of these walls, and an ancient mirrored vanity and a giant armoire were along the other wall.

I wanted to get to work right then, but we had to unpack the car and get ready for bed. It took us until almost midnight to drag the mattresses out of the house and beat the dust out of them with a broom. Then we made the beds with clean linens Mom had brought from home, and we passed out.

The next morning, I woke up before anyone else. It was still dark outside. I walked through the house like I'd lived there all my life. I knew where everything was. It was blueprinted on my brain. I went out the living room door and found another wonder waiting for me. There was a screened porch that ran across the front of the house too. It faced the lake. The sun was just coming up over the water, and inch by inch, I saw the world light up before me. The yard was enclosed on three sides by a stone fence about two-feet high. Through all the weeds and overgrown shrubs, I saw a gorgeous lawn sloping to the water's edge. I'll never forget that morning as long as I live. I'd found paradise.

When everyone else got out of bed, we went straight to work. Mom had worried about bringing Joanne and Tiffany along because we had so much to do. She shouldn't have. I don't know how we could have managed without them. We started at the top of the house and worked our way down. We dusted the ceilings, scrubbed windows, and mopped and polished the wooden floors to a shine. At one point, we thought we'd lost Brandy, but we found her in the armoire. She said she was "the Indian in the cupboard" and rolled out laughing like a hyena. I put her to work scrubbing the toilet and the old claw-foot tub in the bathroom downstairs. She likes scrubbing bathrooms. God only knows why.

Mom started in the kitchen, of course. By noon, she had that old kitchen looking like an ad in a 1950s *Good Housekeeping* magazine. She'd found all kinds of neat kitchen gadgets stowed away in the cabinets, and she had them out on display. She'd sat a big blue-and-white speckled bowl in the middle of the table and filled it with green apples. Even the old checkered curtains came to life with a little dusting and some safety pins.

We cleaned until about 3:00 and then went swimming in the lake. I don't think cold, clear water ever felt so good as it did that day. By evening, we were ready to kick back at the kitchen table and play games. There was a stack to choose from. Joanne had discovered them in the hall closet. Monopoly, checkers, jigsaw puzzles, cards, and Scrabble. It took us 30 minutes just to decide what we wanted to play first.

After two days of cleaning, the real fun began. On Monday, Joanne, Tiffany, and I tackled the back porch. We dug through heaps of discarded stuff and found: three Adirondack chairs, a hammock, paint, brushes, fishing poles, tackle, and a trunk with old handmade quilts. We painted the Adirondack chairs white and put them on the front porch. Then we strung the hammock in a corner and set up my telescope. Joanne said the telescope gave the porch a "sophisticated" look. Mom hand-washed the quilts and hung them to dry on a clothesline out back. We cleaned the fishing stuff and hung it on a wooden rack in Mike's room.

Wednesday, Mike had the day off, so he showed up with everything a handyman could need plus every lawn tool imaginable. In just a few hours, he turned the yard from a jungle into a showplace. Then he mended screens and fixed the sagging shutters. He was so pleased with the work we'd done inside that he said this summer my friends could come back and help paint the place. We're going to paint the house white with dark red trim around the windows and dark blue shutters.

The rest of the week, we played. Mom claimed one of the Adirondack chairs as her very own and sat on the porch with one eye on a book and one on us every afternoon while we swam in the lake or hiked around in the surrounding woods. Tiffany taught us how to rig a fishing pole, so one evening we set out to the water's edge, determined to bring home dinner. Brandy caught a tiny little perch and cried because the hook "poked his mouth." So we let him go and came home empty-handed. Mom said Mike is quite a fisherman. Maybe he can give us some tips for next time.

Thursday
March 20
Joanne

Spending spring break with Sage and Tiffany at the lake has given me a lot to think about. The little house that we stayed in belongs to Sage's mom's boyfriend. It certainly needs a ton of work, but it has potential. I mean, with a little paint and some decorating, it will be a cute vacation cottage. While we were there, I couldn't help but wonder what Sky would say about a place like that. She'd call it a shack and make fun of it, no doubt. And I'm sure she'd rather chew aluminum foil than spend spring break beating the dust out of mattresses and scrubbing floors.

The difference between my new friends and my old ones is the way they look at things. Sage sees an old rundown house as an opportunity to create something beautiful. She sees piles of discarded junk as treasures just waiting for paint and polish. Sky, on the other hand, would look at the house and all of its possessions as nothing more than fuel for a bonfire.

Sky has always had her treasure brought to

her with paint and polish already applied. Maybe that's why she can't dream like Sage can. I mean, Sage isn't poor by any means, but she hasn't had so much in life that she can't appreciate little things. She creates her world from whatever she can find around her. I've always hung around with people who thought a great time was hanging out at the mall with Daddy's credit card. Who would have thought that kids our age could have so much fun playing board games, swimming, hiking, or painting old deck chairs? My new friends have opened my eyes to a whole new world of possibilities. I can do anything, make anything, be anything that I want. All it takes is an imagination and a lot of hard work.

Monday
March 24
Sky

Guess where I spent my spring break? While Candice was off parasailing in Cancun, I was stuck in the nut house. Can you believe it? Daddy had me committed because I refused to eat. Well, you would think that while that hospital was bleeding my parents of money, I'd get some decent treatment. But, OH NO! The doctors were crazier than the patients—or should I say *inmates*. That's how I was treated—like an inmate in a loony bin. The nurses were rude, and my so-called therapist told Momma and Daddy that I have Narcissistic Personality Disorder. Daddy said that means I'm "incurably selfish."

I spent the whole week in a room with a flake named Pamela who is really and truly starving herself. She doesn't even sneak an Almond Joy every now and then. No, Pamela flat-out refuses to eat. And not for a cause or anything, just because she thinks she's fat. For God's sake, how vain! Pamela couldn't get a bite down no matter how much the nurses begged and pleaded. So when they left our trays in the room, I picked at my own food and devoured Puny Pamela's. It caused quite a stir at first. You should have seen the old biddy in charge of our wing. She just about wet herself the first time she saw Pamela's tray licked clean. I had to pull the sheet over my face to keep them from seeing me laugh. Pamela had been miraculously cured, and I had a belly full of ham and black-eyed peas. It took them two whole days to figure out that Pamela wasn't the one doing the eating. That's when they sent me home.

So here I am, back in poverty. After months of sneaking around grabbing food from wherever I could find it, spending spring break in a mental ward, and losing my beautiful figure, I didn't get one thing I wanted. Daddy is still selling the house, Momma is still driving the minivan, and I have dishwater hands. At least I'm getting my figure back. I'm eating like a horse. Why not? As they say, the gig is up.

chapter 9

April

Corner Girl faces out
Overcomes her inner doubt
Sister's dead, not returning
Parents' hearts forever yearning.

Will recover
Time will heal
Memories live
Forever real.

Joshua

Tuesday
April 1
Sage

I'm obsessed. I can't think of anything but the lake house. Joanne gave me a stack of decorating magazines that her mother was going to throw away. Miss Laughinghouse caught me with one of them stuck between the pages of my language arts book. We were supposed to be reviewing indirect objects, but I was looking at a great picture of a living room painted blue with a wallpaper border of sailboats and lighthouses. She took the magazine. I hope she gives it back at the end of the year. I wanted that picture for my collection. I'm gathering ideas for lake-house projects.

Mike told me that he's going to hire me as his decorator this summer and that he'll buy all the materials that I need to fix the place up. At first, I was so excited I couldn't even think straight, but then I got to worrying. What if Mike and Mom don't stay together? Does Mike think I'm getting too attached to the house? Is that why he offered to pay me to fix it up? Is he afraid I'm starting to think of it as mine? All of these questions are tainting my excitement. If I learned anything from Mom and Dad's divorce, I learned that the bottom can drop out of your life at any moment. I have to be prepared for the worst.

Saturday
April 12
Tiffany

I woke up this morning feeling gloomy. Today is the second anniversary of Marilyn's death. We had to go to the cemetery and leave flowers on her grave. I dreaded it from the moment I opened my eyes. I don't want to relive the whole tragedy. I remember the funeral like it was yesterday. Weird things like the brown petals on a bouquet of chrysanthemums by the casket. The way Reverend Delaplane's tie hung a little to the left. Details. Odd things. I try not to think about that day, ever. Going to the cemetery makes all the memories come flooding back. Like when you wake up from a nightmare and no matter how hard you try to think of something else, the monsters keep popping back in your mind to scare you all over again.

We went after lunch. Everyone was tense. We rode all the way there in silence. I tried to think about anything but where we were going. I hate the cemetery. I have a picture of Marilyn in my mind. She's in the kitchen trying to teach Mom how to do the bump and grind and laughing her head off. That picture has nothing to do with the image I get at the cemetery. I don't want to think of my sister as a molding corpse six feet under a mound of dirt. I don't know why we even have to go there. What does that place have to do with Marilyn, really?

When we got there, we walked past all the other graves to Marilyn's. Every one of these people represent someone's family gone awry. There are little tiny graves with stone cherubs guarding them—someone's baby. Double graves—someone's grandma and grandpa or mom and dad. It's the most depressing place in the world.

At Marilyn's grave, Mom got busy arranging flowers. Dad stood to the side with his hands folded in front of him, staring at the headstone like he was still shocked to see his daughter's name in pink granite. I stood next to him, feeling awkward and guilty for being alive. Then without thinking about it, I reached over and took Dad's hand. He squeezed my fingers, looked at me, and smiled. Not a sad, grief-stricken smile, but a "Hey, kid. I'll race you to the car" smile. And that's what we did. We turned around and raced back to the old Taurus Wagon. It was a tie; we hit the hood at the same time. I turned around breathless and laughing, and there was Mom. She was almost smiling.

We talked all the way home. Not about sad things, either. We each told our favorite Marilyn memory. Mine, of course, was dirty dancing in the kitchen. Mom's was the time Marilyn was ten and gave mouth-to-mouth to a kitten she found drowning in the neighbor's ditch. We still have the cat. His name's Bosley, and he's almost 11 years old. Dad's memory was the best. He told us about taking Marilyn to the hospital to see me the day I was born. How she stroked my hair and played with my fingers. I didn't know it until today, but Marilyn cried the first time she saw me. She was so happy to have a baby sister.

THURSDAY
APRIL 17
BRANDON

Pop bought me a car. How 'bout that for fatherly love? It's a red '85 Mustang GT with a hot 5.0 five-speed and nitrous oxide. Awesome wheels. One of his buddies from the VFW sold it to him for 500 bucks. His son started to build it as a racecar and then ran off to Seattle to be a Nirvana groupie. That was back when Kurt Cobain was still alive, if that tells you how long the car's been sitting. His loss—Kurt's dead and I got a kickin' ride. It doesn't run yet, but it will. The suspension and interior are shot, so I'm putting in as much time as I can at the theater to earn the cash for bushings, shocks, struts, and an interior kit. I found the interior I wanted in *Hot Rod Magazine*. It's black. The chicks won't be able to resist me once I'm cruisin' down Main with my Rockford Fosgate Punch 400s with twin crossovers, megabass, and six-disc CD changer thumpin' out tunes.

Pop said he and I would get to work on the car as soon as school lets out for summer. He said he built his first car when he was 14, and he and his dad used to race out at Shady Oaks Speedway back in the '50s when it was a hot place to hang. Now it's somebody's cow pasture. He's all wound up about getting the car on the road. We sit in the living room at night and make parts lists. I figure I'll need at least 1500 bones just to get the basics and another grand for the stereo—minimum. But come summer, I can work just about every night at the theater, and Pop said he'd pitch in a couple hundred here and there if I help him cut up some of the old junk cars and get 'em out of the yard. Mom's been pitching a fit to get some of that crap cleaned up so she can plant a garden. Now that Pop quit drinking and got a job, Mom doesn't have to clean other people's houses anymore. Suddenly she's gotten awful particular about ours. "No feet on the coffee table. Put your underwear in the laundry basket. Scrape your plate. Wipe your shoes." She even bosses old Pop around. A regular drill sergeant. But, that's cool. Whatever puts a smile on Mom's face is okay by me.

Monday
April 28
Tiffany

Mom couldn't wait to get me out of the house this weekend. She kept telling me that I should "get out and have some fun." That usually means, "Your dad and I want to have some time alone." So, I called Sage, and we went bumming around town. We went to a sidewalk sale at Wal-Mart that had absolutely nothing that kids would be interested in. There were just a bunch of old people milling around looking at garden gloves and weed-eaters. Then we killed an hour eating Blizzards at Dairy Queen. We hit a few garage sales while we were walking around town. Sage is on a quest for "good junk" to decorate the lake house.

When we ran out of places to go, we walked to my house, thinking we'd pick up a few movies and take them to Joanne's. Mom had locked all the doors, so I had to knock. She wouldn't even let me in the house to get the movies. She said she and Dad were "busy." I didn't know what they were busy doing, but Sage and I laughed about the possibilities all the way to Joanne's.

Sage and I ended up spending the night at Joanne's. When I came home Sunday night, Mom made me close my eyes and put my hand over my face while she led me through the house. After bumping into every piece of furniture we owned, she finally stopped and yelled "SURPRISE!" I opened my eyes to find myself in front of Marilyn's bedroom door. Mom threw it open, and there were all my things. My bed, my stereo, posters, books, everything. It's my room now. Even the bathroom. All mine.

There was a box on my bed with "Tiffany" written in big black letters. In it were some of Marilyn's things that Mom thought I might like to have. There was a poetry book by Jewel, a box of pictures, some stationary, Marilyn's old diary, and at the bottom of the box, all of the notebook paper and pens that she'd left in her desk that last weekend she was home. I looked through the pictures first. They were mostly of Marilyn and her friends. Pictures from when Marilyn was my age. I discovered that Marilyn wasn't always the gorgeous prom queen. In junior high, she needed braces and wore tiny little wire frame glasses. Funny, I'd always remembered Marilyn as beautiful. I guess that's because she was so much older than me.

Anyway, the best thing in the box was Marilyn's diary. The first paragraph said, "When I grow up, I want to be a movie star, but I'm ugly so I'll have to play the parts nobody else wants. My smile is hideous, and my arms are so skinny that my hands look like they belong to someone else. I always wear long sleeves, even when it's hot, because I don't want anyone to see my skinny wrists." I closed the diary and got the pictures back out of the box. Sure enough, there was Marilyn at the Fourth of July parade wearing a windbreaker. Marilyn and I weren't so different. She felt awkward and insecure about herself too. It made me sad to think that I'd never really known Marilyn until now.

I only read two pages. I'm going to read a little of the diary every day. It's like listening to my big sister tell me about when she was my age. I want it to last awhile.

chapter 10

May

Geometric plane. Flexible band.
Sharpened pencil by my hand.
Perfect pattern. Undisturbed.
Rigid wood and rubber curve.
What's the answer? There it lies.
Perfect pattern in my eyes.

Joshua

Sage

Miss Laughinghouse wants us to write our final entry on what we learned this year. Well, here goes. I learned that people aren't perfect. Not even parents. My dad did some things that could be considered unforgivable. But he is my dad, and I love him anyway. The divorce hurt me beyond words, but I suppose it was even worse for Mom. She couldn't keep it together for me and Brandy or even for herself. I learned that parents aren't any more immune to pain than kids. Most of the time they're better at dealing with it, but not always. Moms and dads are human like everyone else.

I also learned that life goes on in spite of the moment, and change can be a good thing. Mike and Mom are engaged. I feel a little guilty because I'm so happy about it. I like Mike. I think I've said that before. He's great. When I see Mom with Mike, I realize that she's really happy now. I took the old photo album out of my closet. In the pictures of us as a family, before the divorce, I see something in Mom's face that I hadn't noticed before. She looked strained. Like her smile was just there for the camera. Now she's really smiling. And Dad and Carly look really happy too.

I thought about starting a new album of post-divorce pictures. But I changed my mind. There are plenty of pages in the old one. I got my box of glue and Exacto knives out of the closet and started putting in pictures from Dad and Carly's reception party. Tonight, I'll add pictures of the lake house. After all, this is my life. It started out with Mom, Dad, me, and Brandy. Now we have Carly and Mike. Things have changed, and maybe we're not the ideal family, but we are a family, and that will never change.

BRANDON

It'd be easier for me to say what I didn't learn this year than it would be to say what I did learn. That's because I have it all spelled out for me on my progress report. According to The Tank, I didn't learn one "iota of history." Mr. Silva says, "I have a knack for butchering the Spanish language that even surpasses my knack for butchering English." And you, Miss Laughinghouse, say I can't write a decent sentence or speak a whole thought without throwing in "slang and profanity." So, there it is: Brandon McCormick is illiterate.

But that goes to show what you people know about education. From the day I was born, I've been in perfect attendance at the University of Life. I never forget a lesson. The first thing I learned in school was never to let teachers think you're smart. If you do, they'll have all kinds of high expectations for you. Then if you want to take a break from academia, they get all blown out and hassle you about not living up to your potential. So, teachers, I pulled one over on you all. I learned plenty in the seventh grade. I learned:

1. Reading: If you want to badger a blonde brat, make sure she doesn't have a beefy boyfriend. That's alliteration, a poetic device.
2. History: Civil war is a no-win proposition. Examples: U.S.A., Korea, Vietnam, and Pop and Brandon McCormick.
3. Spanish: Enough to insult non-Spanish-speaking jerks who cut in front of me at an amusement park and to read assembly instructions when I spilled a glass of Coke on the English version.

4. Language arts: Laughinghouse, notice my flawless use of punctuation, complete sentences, and lack of profanity. I hope you learned something from this!

Tiffany

I'm getting braces next month. No more buck teeth. I'm also getting my hair cut, and Mom said Joanne could put highlights in it for the summer. Treiu and I broke up. We're still pen pals, but the long-distance relationship thing wasn't working out. I'm not devastated or anything. Next year, I'll be in the eighth grade, and I don't want to be tied down to a boyfriend that lives so far away.

I'm supposed to say what I learned this year. If I could sum it all up, I'd say that I learned to like myself. I don't know exactly how that happened. Making friends certainly had a lot to do with it. But it was more than that. I took a good look at other people and realized that we all have something wrong with us. It's just that some things are easier to hide than others. The hardest thing for me to hide wasn't my buck teeth and messy hair, but my bad attitude about myself. Reading Marilyn's diary helped me get over that. Knowing that Marilyn, who I envied more than anyone, had gone through the same things I had. She'd felt insecure and ugly too. Sometimes we're our own worst critics. Sure, there are always going be people like Sky, who is a master at spotting other people's insecurities so she can throw them in their face. But most people just saw me as a shy girl who would rather read than talk.

Now when I'm at school, I hold my head up and smile at people—without putting my hand in front of my teeth. People smile back. They talk to me. They ask me where I bought my jeans, how I did on my Spanish test, if I'm going to the pool this weekend, all kinds of things. It's amazing. I spent every school day for the last eight years staring at the ground, certain that if I looked up, everyone would be laughing or staring at me. Now I know that most people were just going on with their own lives, too busy to worry about whether Tiffany's hair was frizzy or her teeth stuck out. I see kids like me in the hall hiding behind their open locker door, and I make a point of walking up to them and saying something nice. Sometimes they gawk at me like I'm from Mars, but most of the time they look surprised and smile.

As I write this, Marilyn is grinning at me from two framed pictures on my desk. In one, she has braces and is wearing a blue windbreaker; in the other, she's flawless in a sequined prom dress. I wish I could tell her how proud I am to be her little sister.

Sky

Miss Goofy Laughinghouse insists that we write our final journal entry on "what we learned in the seventh grade." Well, let me tell you, I learned a whole lot.

First and foremost, I learned that most people are delusional. They wouldn't know the truth if it sneaked up behind them and bit them on the butt. Everywhere I look, I see someone living a lie because they don't want to face reality. Take Daddy for instance. All the time we were living high, oblivious to the fact that he was losing his shirt. If he'd had the sense to let Momma know what was going on, she could have done something about it. Momma is a wonderful money manager. But, oh no, he just kept letting us spend money like there was no tomorrow, and then—POW! We're in the poor house. All because Daddy couldn't look life full in the face and admit that he wasn't everything he thought he was.

And Daddy isn't the only one who lives in a fantasy world. Joanne never did figure out that she was just a lowly pawn in John Keeler's plan to make me jealous. That judge took the word of a deranged jock and a retard over mine, when any moron could see that I was the only honest person in that courtroom. Even Tiffany Andrews suddenly thinks she's a somebody. She walked past me in the hall today, looked me right in the eyes, and asked, "How's it going, Sky?" The nerve of her. Can't people take a good look in the mirror and make an honest assessment of themselves? Daddy is a loser, Joanne is a wanna-be from a third-world country, that judge is an idiot, and Tiffany Andrews is an ugly little nobody. To sum it up, I have learned that, with the exception of Momma, I am the only person on the face of this earth who has a clue.

I have also learned that honesty and integrity are rewarded by a higher power. Next week we're moving into our new house. It's small, only three bedrooms, and it doesn't have a pool. But it's right next door to the Keelers'. Some may call this coincidence; I call it fate. I will win John Keeler because it is my destiny and my compensation for suffering. Then when he's so in love with me that he can't stand it, I'll break his heart in two and leave him writhing in pain like he deserves. Life is a game, and I, Sky Davis, will always come out a winner.

Joanne

Poor John. Yesterday he was in the front yard washing his dad's car when Sky and her mother pulled into the driveway next door. Sky jumped out of the van and yelled, "Howdy neighbor." John said he just about dropped his sponge and ran for the front door. She came flouncing over to him wearing hiking boots and jeans with a copy of *War and Peace* tucked under her arm. She said she wanted to get together with him later in the summer to discuss the book. She "just couldn't make heads or tails of all that Russian history." John told her that she'd be better off asking his dad since he's the professor and John's never even read *War and Peace.* How obvious can you get? Hiking boots and huge volumes of 19th-century literature are not part of Sky's usual ensemble. Oh, well. She may as well end the year the same way she started it, making a complete fool of herself.

This year I learned that people are not always what they seem to be. That some people are rotten to the core without exception or apology. I think that must be some kind of mental illness. Or maybe there is an essential element left out of some people and because it was never there, they don't know it's missing. I think about all the time I spent with Sky, and I can't remember one time that she did anything that wasn't self-serving. I've never even seen her be nice without a motive. The sad thing is that if someone tried to explain that to her, she wouldn't understand what on earth they were talking about. It would be like describing the color red to a blind man.

I must have noticed that Sky was crazy back when we were friends, but I guess I just ignored it because being with Sky was the price I paid for being popular. Not only did I hang out with someone mean, I did other things that are worse. I became mean too. I laughed at other kids, I showed bigotry toward my own culture, and I was a snob. If it hadn't been for Sage and Tiffany, I might still be that way. Hanging out with them reminded me of when I lived in the city, before we moved here. There were so many kids there that I didn't even try to be popular. Who would have noticed? I liked myself then, and I like myself now. I had to learn the hard way that being popular isn't nearly as much fun as being me.